THE
THIRTEENTH
MONTH

THE THIRTEENTH MONTH

COLIN HAMILTON

Black
Lawrence
Press

Black
Lawrence
Press

www.blacklawrence.com

Executive Editor: Diane Goettel
Book and Cover Design: Amy Freels
Cover Art: "IR Amazonia Arvore e menino sentado" by Betina Samaia

Published 2019 by Black Lawrence Press.
Printed in the United States.

For Theo & Will

Do you know what the worst thing about literature is? said Don Pancracio.
I knew, but I pretended I didn't.
—Roberto Bolaño

Contents

Part One

CALL IT COURAGE

So that I'd think of her each day, my mom taped a photo of her new home to the mirror above my dresser. She was living in little shack balanced among the branches of a tree. It was the kind of sanctuary I'd often dreamed of having hidden deep in our backyard, a place I could disappear into with a stack of comics, but rather than a sky-ascending Iowan oak, her tree was twisted, half stripped of bark, and it leaned out over the muddy banks of a lagoon. A ladder had been hammered into its trunk, and at the top of the ladder a screen door sat unevenly in its frame. Behind that screen everything was dark, but I could imagine her there writing the letters that would arrive every few days.

It was my sister's job to read them aloud while my dad made dinner. My mom wrote about the strange feasts she and the others made of crabs they caught by hand and boiled in creek water. She wrote about a clever pig named Musgrove that liked to rummage in the muck beneath her treehouse. She described their favorite swimming hole, which they'd clear of alligators by singing loudly and thrashing the marsh grasses with sticks. Sometimes an ornery old beast would refuse to budge, in which case they'd have to swim on the far side of the water while he lurked perfectly still in the mud with just his speckled eyes tracking them. It was quite safe, she assured us, as long as they could see the gator sunning himself on the other side of the cove, hopefully dazed by a little deer digesting in his swollen lizard belly. She wrote that she was very, very happy.

While my mom was away, I did the usual things, setting off on my bike to find my friend Steve or the twins, Nick and Dan, and we'd band together to explore the woody ravines that cut through our neighborhood. There we'd stage elaborate battles between armies of green and grey plastic soldiers, splattering them with napalm-inspired model airplane glue and setting them alight to our cheers of rat-a-tat-tat. As the sun rose higher, some adult would feed us lunch, and then invariably we'd end up at the pool, which was just down the hill and through a park from my house, our backs salty and red.

But evenings were different. After a game of kickball in the street or ghost in the graveyard through the interlocked backyards, I'd come home. When my mom was there, she'd always be the first to bed, always with a book, and I was welcome beside her if I brought one of my own, a clever lure as reading was something of a torment for me, laboring through books that others consumed in a gulp. But there, next to her, it didn't matter. If the words were a jumble, if the letters leapt back and forth mockingly, I still had my mom. Now, though, the bed was empty. My dad mostly spent his evenings with Chaucer or Montaigne, but he preferred to read upright in his study, with a glass of scotch and the freedom to wander the darkened halls of our home, typically naked, something we never discussed but which I always assumed had to do with having grown up on a farm.

When she left for Ossabaw—that was the name of it, a sandy island buffering the Georgia coast from tropical storms where she'd retreated with a colony of artists—my mom gave me a book she said I would enjoy, *Call It Courage*, and asked me to write to her about it when I was finished. Unlike the usual flimsy paperback of my youth, this was a hardcover wrapped with a rough canvas and stamped by the intimidating, totemic marks of Pacific Island tattoos. I put it off for weeks, but finally one night, curled up alone in the cave of my bottom bunk, I made myself begin. Like most of the stories I knew, this one was about a young boy, but rather than a future French knight or secret English prince, he lived on a remote Pacific island surrounded by the crashing waves. The children all played in the tides except for Mafatu, that was his name, who was terrified of the water because

when he was just a toddler his mother had taken him out into the ocean
to hunt sea urchins when a terrible storm descended, and although she'd
managed to save her son, she was swept out to sea and drowned. He grew
up surrounded by the taunting waves that had claimed his mom. Amongst
a people who made their living fishing and trading between islands, it was
a terrible shame to fear the water, and he was ridiculed for his cowardice,
taunted by other boys, motherless, an embarrassment to his father, and
ultimately the elders couldn't even bring themselves to look at him.

As I read, alone in the dark, I could picture her swimming in her
muddy lagoon, the alligator's slow and devouring gaze upon her; I could
picture those clouds darkening into a storm and the still lagoon water
beginning to churn. Why had she given me such a horrible book? Mafatu
was a coward, and I felt all the things he was feeling. Was that what she
was trying to tell me? Had she seen, as only a mother could, how my fragile
soul recoiled from every challenge? If it had been a school night, my father
would have eventually responded to the beacon light in my room, come to
me and discovered my dismay, but it was summer, and he was lost in pages
of his own; if he noticed the light at all, he was probably proud to believe I
had stayed up late reading.

Since sleep was impossible, and perhaps more frightening than the
known darkness of my room, I had no choice but to keep going, just as
Mafatu did when he could no longer stand the taunts and humiliations
and decided to face his fears by setting off into the murderous sea in his
little canoe, accompanied only by his dog and a pet albatross. Doon, my
loyal canine companion, was curled at my feet, in theory guarding me from
dangers though unaware that they weren't sneaking in through the window but between the covers of a book. In another storm, Mafatu loses his
sail, mast, and all their provisions, and the trio is left adrift over waters
full of dark, silent forms glimmering beneath them. Eventually they are
washed ashore on an island, which he recognizes by the scattered bones as
belonging to the dreaded Eaters of Men. He knows they should push back
into the waves, but they are starving and thirsty. He steals a spear from a
sacred, bloodied site and uses it to fend off a wild boar and then to kill a

tiger shark—bold acts for a cowardly boy. Discovered by the cannibals, the trio barely escapes back into the sea in their shallow canoe, wandering again until they finally wash ashore back at their own island, where all the villagers rush to welcome them and Mafatu is accepted at last by his father as a brave and admirable son.

It would be, she explained, very important that we write each other frequent letters while she was away and that I told her as much as I could about my life. She promised to do the same. Her own father, she added, had written her a letter every year on her birthday, assembling a collection that became, over time, one of her most prized possessions. "Over time" was a key phrase, because she didn't find the letters until after he'd died. He chose to keep them to himself, presumably, because many of the things he wanted to say were ambiguous at best, such as confessing in the very first of his letters that he'd never particularly wanted kids. On her eighth birthday, he wrote: "You are still growing up. And you are still frequently difficult, explosive, and sometimes scatter-brained. But you have a swell bump of curiosity, and during the past year you have devoted a lot of attention to the birds and flowers around your new home. Today I think you know more about flowers than I have ever known. The simple truth is you can be very, very nice, and increasingly often you are." On her sixteenth birthday, he added: "This growing maturity also shows in your reasonably frequent letters home, which are interesting, very amusing, and well written—in spite of the fact that you apparently have not heard of punctuation."

I didn't write to her about *Call It Courage* because I had no idea what to say. Instead my letters said little at all. The score of a soccer match. That I helped my dad pick walnuts from the yard so he could mow without them exploding into fragrant, staining shards under the gas-powered blade. But when she finally returned with the first days of fall, she found it sitting by my bedside—an unavoidable prop when she came to kiss me goodnight. "Did you ever read it?" she asked innocently. Although I had been obsessing about it for weeks and had been bracing for this crushing exchange, I realized instantly she had forgotten it entirely. And with that I burst into tears, to her great confusion. Between sobs and shakes, I explained what a horrible book it was, that I thought she had drowned, that she thought I was a coward, and she, utterly confused, assured me that she had no idea that it was about dead mothers and cowardly sons. Someone had simply suggested it as a good book for boys.

For my mom, reading and travel were intimately connected. She loved the letters and memoirs of fearless women, Mary Kingsley, Gertrude Bell, and Freya Stark, who with properly buttoned collars and wide-brimmed hats managed to be carried through Africa or to cross the Middle East by camel without missing tea, and although it took most of her life to make that leap herself, she would eventually ride a bike through the Valley of Kings and negotiate the markets of Mali. Despite, or perhaps because of her almost pathological fear of the cold, she loved tales of polar expeditions, especially those that failed, especially those of handsome, doomed Ernest Shackleton, and some nights when I couldn't sleep, she'd lie beside me and tell me about the sounds his ships had made being cracked open like nuts wedged between sheets of ice, or about what it must have been like for him in the unrelenting dark to chew on shoe leather to soothe his hunger. Any story with a little taste of death to it, somehow that calmed her.

It must have calmed me too, I suppose, because I began to collect in a discarded prescription vial a haphazard cocktail of aspirin, decongestants, anti-depressants and sleeping pills I'd pillaged from our house's varied cabinets. As the vial filled, I could feel my own anxiety lessening. I knew or at least believed that if things, mysterious Things, should ever become too bad, I had, clever boy, devised my own escape hatch. That vial hidden at the back of a drawer, a little charm, would keep me safe—not from death but from an excess of life. My mom and I might have been mesmerized by those who sucked their last meal out of a rotten shoe sole, but that kind of struggle wasn't for us. It wasn't any great surprise when she eventually took her own life.

As a little girl, she'd once journeyed along the top of a stone wall that circled the local zoo's bear den. When her sister shouted, she slipped and fell into their pit, knocking the wind from her lungs. Two huge bears, dark and lumbering, were grooming themselves at the far side of the dugout, and startled by this sudden, little intruder, they lurched to their feet to investigate. Throughout her days, my mom could remember their yellowy eyes and her own bottomless fear as she tried to suck the air back into her chest. Then the cries as a uniformed zookeeper leapt into the pit, waving his arms to fend off the great beasts, and lifting this little girl up into her father's arms.

Late in his life, as deafness made her father increasingly remote and my mom struggled to find any conversation to engage him, she reminded him of the story of the bear pit, and she shared how throughout her life she'd often thought about his rescue, how, as long as he lived, she never doubted everything would be ok. He just smiled a little absently and said, "You know that never actually happened, don't you?" And although she was in the prime of life and he was sinking into dementia, she knew he was right.

Her father, we called him Far, was full of surprises, like the fact that he had taught himself to write in Japanese or that he kept a small pistol in his desk. His wife, "*Christine!*" as he called her, on the other hand, was mostly full of Virginia Gentleman, a low-end bourbon that was hidden behind books, under linens and sofas and at the backs of cabinets throughout their house. Christine Kleisus had been one of the prettier girls in Altoona, Pennsylvania when they met, and undoubtedly she made perfect sense for his ambitions when he was a mere junior account manager, but she became a painful embarrassment as he rose, which he in turn made painfully clear to her, and his authoritarian disdain unleashed all of our worst instincts. My sister, cousins, and I referred to her as The Claw, because when she would touch us in a failed imitation of affection, it was as though a heavy bird of prey, a vulture, was digging its talons into the soft flesh around our collarbones, and we could only respond by recoiling. Her daughters, thoroughly overwhelmed, maddened, and cared for by their dad, focused all their rebelliousness on disapproving of their mother.

A few years after my parents' divorce, my mom and her new husband hosted a Christmas party, and from their front window I watched my widowed Granny shuffle along the brick walkway through a gate to their townhome with a large, unwieldy holiday platter in her arms. Just then my mom called me from the kitchen to hand her the wooden spoon that sat just out of her reach as she stirred some sauce—a defining, narcissistic habit of hers, asking for unnecessary help simply to make sure that I was sufficiently focused on whatever she was doing, complicit. When I returned to the window, I saw Granny had fallen down a flight of six brick steps and was lying flat on her back on the icy walk.

I must have cried out, but what I remember is dashing out the door and to her side. She was moving just ever so slightly, mechanically, muttering but clearly unconscious. I held her hand and tried to say comforting things into the void where she had receded. The back of her head, which had struck the sidewalk, was bleeding and pools of thick, sticky blood were gathering around her; some of it soaked through my pants and clutched my knee. Despite the release, her face was visibly swelling. My mom was then beside us both. "I think that's German," she said, trying to interpret what might be Granny's final words but which, like so much else she had said over the years, was misunderstood and forgotten. As time slowly regained its pulse, what had been a single, all-consuming instant began to creep forward into aching minutes while we waited for help and began to feel the cold air snake around us.

In the ambulance, my mom remained quite calm, conversing with the EMS team and then the doctors and nurses as they stabilized Granny into a coma, with a mask pushing air into her lungs and a maze of tubes circulating yellowish, antique fluids. After a while, there was nothing more to do and we cabbed back to my mom's house where the Christmas party had gone along without us, with rounds of drinks, a roast, sugars and pie. Through most of the afternoon I'd been crying on and off, in unexpected bursts and sad little whimpers, and although I'd been ashamed of my first, most overwhelming release, I also felt a flash of fierce pride that I had been brought to tears by my grandmother's possible death while my family pretended it had no choice but to set out the appetizers and pop the bubbly, even though I secretly knew my tears had not been out of grief for dear old Granny but simply in response to the sheer horribleness of it all, the adrenaline and the fear. My aunt Douglass, who always confused me by being a quite beautiful, less-directly related version of my mom but also smelling a bit like the goats she raised on a little farm outside of Philadelphia, embraced me and did her best to look serious. "Do you think she'll make it?" she asked, wrinkling her nose, a gesture meant to convey concern but one remarkably close to disgust.

"I, I don't know... I think she might die," I whimpered, slipping back into my tears.

She handed me a champagne flute. "Well," she said, clinking her own against mine, "that's too bad."

But it had never been Granny's way to make things easy on others, especially her daughters. Through several visits to the hospital over the following days, they did their best to look grave for the doctors while deciding that the time had come to pull the plug. In a misguided attempt to comfort an upset nurse, my mom joked that her own living will read that if she ever got a bad cold, she didn't want to be revived. Whatever relief they felt walking away from Granny's bedside, driving away from the hospital, feeling closer to one another than they had in years by swapping traumatizing stories from their adolescence to great nervous laughter, whatever momentary ecstasy they found was gnawed away and replaced by something harder to digest over the coming days as Granny's unplugged and unaided but tough old heart, that vulgar little beast, continued to beat.

MONOLITHOS

It is August, always August. The brown Iowa River has slowed to a thick, chemical drift; the grass as bleached as all the girls' hair, golden and stiff. My skin is burned and peeling, raw in the hot, heavy air. The parents have disappeared—into air-conditioned offices or far, secret reaches of our homes—leaving us children to fend for ourselves at the pool, on our bikes, against cool basement walls.

In the mornings I get myself up early and still half-asleep walk down our long, straight street to the corner where I wait for and then catch the city bus. It carries me across town to my tutor, a retired classics professor who is supposed to teach me Latin in the hope that learning word roots will help untangle the dyslexic jumble in my head. For months now I've been studying the nominative, dative, accusative, and genitive cases. Years later, when I have forgotten almost all of this, a friend will tell me that the true beauty of Latin is that every sentence can mean what it says, the exact opposite, or something obscene, and I'll think that maybe I did learn something after all.

The bus shudders as it stops to swallow me up. The driver is always the same heavy-set man slowly melting into the vinyl bowl of the driver's seat, his upper half dissolving into streams of sweat even here in the early morning. He greets me warmly, as though he's been waiting for me, storing up the bad jokes he can't wait to share. "Hey kid," he says as I drop my quarter, "do you know why you can't hear a pterodactyl going to the bathroom?" I take my usual seat a few rows back—too far away for him to speak to me without shouting over the engine but near enough to remain within his within his sight. "The P is silent," he calls back. To keep him on my side, I make sure he sees me smile in his mirror. He winks.

The bus rolls down a slope, past the park, the pool, the art school. Across the river it ascends Dubuque Street and the heart of campus. At the tail end of summer, riders are few and far between, mostly stray students who for one reason or another never went home. I watch one in a grey athletic t-shirt come down the aisle, with his slightly bowed legs and his broad shoulders tipped forward, elbows winged back. He seems overly alert, ready—but for what? He sits in the row one in front and across from me. His hair is cut short and thoughtlessly, his jawline studded with pimples, his left ear both swollen and mashed into his head. His sits perfectly still but for his one jiggling leg. It is hard to say which is winning, this relentless energy inside him or his powerful self-control. Although he is small for a man, I can sense a much larger creature squeezed into his body, trying to get out. When he turns my way, I make sure to keep my gaze straight ahead. I know who, or at least what, he is.

In Iowa City, wrestlers are a bit like tigers at the zoo, a source of both pride and fear. Mostly farm boys from western Iowa, Nebraska, and the Dakotas, they are all-conquering, having won nine consecutive national championships. From mat-side at the arena and the safety of our living rooms where TVs flicker and glow, we've cheered with exorbitant pride as they twisted physically and morally weaker easterners and southerners into knots and pinned them squirming flat. We're never quite sure what to think of those from the golden West but suspect them of some kind of irredeemable frivolousness.

On the playground the more knowing kids explain how our wrestlers—many champions at 125, 133, 141 pounds—cruise the campus bars picking fights with much larger undergrads, who dulled by alcohol make the terrible mistake of thinking their pumped-up physiques will protect them. There are legends of the squad squaring off against the basketball team—virtually all towering black men imported from Chicago, Detroit, and St. Louis—in the late hours of another Saturday night. How it filled our little white minds with joy, with relief, to whisper of their victories.

That my dad, my bookish, professorial dad, had been raised a wrestler imbued him with a thin strand of alien DNA, as did his youth in rural Missouri where his father and uncle had cleared a river bottom farm and made a tough living raising hogs and soybeans, fending off the occasional flood and the persistent banker. While Iowa might seem indistinguishable from Missouri to many, the gulf between a university town and a farming community is vast. At a young age, I'd been taught to juggle a soccer ball but my dad had learned to swing an ax and to saw a straight line, occasionally earning his father's highest praise: "competent." His favorite book had been *Two Little Savages*, a story of farm boys like himself who play Indian for a summer, living off the land and in the wild, "savages" a term of both condescension and envy. When they'd scour recently upturned fields for arrowheads and other relics, they called it "hunting Indians." In another life he would have inherited the farm and all its crushing debts, grown heavy and bitter, but my dad's brutal allergies and hay fever meant that when everyone else was sent out to weed and detassel corn, he'd turn a shade of green and double over wheezing.

Late each summer, obligation would get the better of him and my dad would load us into the station wagon and we'd all turn south to visit his family. We'd drive a long, dusty route through as many back roads as he could find, which he would always claim was the expression of a regional aesthetic but which I ultimately understood as simply being in no hurry to arrive back home.

My grandfather, Ted, was a frightening figure who looked like a cross between a Biblical prophet and Ernest Hemingway, manly and judgmental. One time he greeted me, his first and only male heir, with a motorized model airplane set he'd special ordered from Chicago and together we spent long hours in his workshop, me seated dutifully and observant on a hard wooden stool while he diligently disassembled the myriad pieces, then snapped and glued them together, his eyes moving back and forth between the obscure directions and the half-formed plane. When it was finally finished, the whole family was summoned and we drove out to one of his fields for our test flight, where the plane, on a long string, was to loop in circles around him. Only it failed, either the engine never clicking on or sputtering, dipping, and crashing back to earth after the briefest of launches, at which point my grandfather erupted into a fury of vicious, inventive curses and snapping branches. On another visit, he announced he would take me duck hunting the next morning at five, which filled me with a nervous excitement until I learned as we loaded into his truck, still half-asleep, that it meant he would carry a rifle and I, unarmed, would walk silently behind him through cold marsh grass and learn.

I was always uncomfortable around my Missouri cousins—three older, brash, and knowing girls who'd debate old copies of *Playboy* they'd stolen from their dad's workshop. "What's your type?" they'd prod me. Young forensics, they'd determined their father's favorites by the creased corners and the break of the binding. One day we were wilting together in our grandparents' backyard, our games all stifled to dullness by the oppressive heat when a gunshot ripped by and before our eyes a small rodent was tossed into the air, smoking, and hit the ground, pulsating with its final panicked breaths. We were frozen until my grandfather marched by us, hot rifle at his side, and seized the carcass by its ears. With a commanding gesture, he ushered us to his picnic table, and while we stood in a solemn obedience, he used his pocket knife to split the creature in half, open its stomach and extract some half-digested plant matter. When we failed to understand, he lowered himself to explain, "This rabbit was eating my lettuce." He always called his wife "Bunny."

Independent people, they'd built their modest, midcentury home themselves. Its back deck overlooked the Missouri River, and one of their daily rituals was to ring a loud brass bell as the barges—*American Spirit, Lugger 21, Dixie Valor, Zeus*—passed below, answering with the resounding bellows of their horns. As they cleared flood plains for their expanding farm, my grandfather and his brother had amassed and documented a substantial collection of arrowheads, flint tools, and shards of pottery dating back hundreds of years and spanning multiple cultures. The walls of his house were mounted with Indian bows, pipes, frontier rifles, and other tantalizing artifacts we were not allowed to touch.

He had led an unexpected, secret life—secret in that Midwestern way, not confidential but in the past, and therefore not worth discussing—that I only absorbed in bits and pieces. That, for example, his favorite book was *Walden*, and reading it as a young man had inspired him to abandon a promising career at *The Chicago Tribune* to return to Missouri and the land. Or, even more oddly, that he'd first left home to join the Quaker Relief Service, which sent him to far eastern Poland in the years immediately after the First World War to distribute seeds, farm implements, lumber, and the know-how necessary to rebuild farmlands that had been devastated by invading armies, the subsequent revolution, and famines. Although they must have been burdensome, he brought along a Corona typewriter and a Kodak camera so he could document his travels, perhaps planning his great novel. In one of his first letters home, he reassured his parents that among the Poles, two of the best known and most admired Americans were fellow Missourians, Mark Twain and Jesse James, and as part of their company, he'd been welcomed graciously. Though it took four decades, he finally recorded his adventures in a book, *The Aftermath of War: Experiences of a Quaker Relief Officer on the Polish-Russian Border*.

A copy was visible on our shelves throughout my childhood, but there was some piece of me that never deigned to take an interest until one bored afternoon not so long after his death. The prose, written many years after the events themselves and largely repeating the flow of his letters home, invites a half-attentive skim, but the book is also filled by black and white photographs, the blacks heavy and impenetrable, the whites a hazy grey. With his practical eye, many capture what work or daily life meant in the aftermath of war, timber rafts on the Dnieper-Bug Canal or a peasant with his homemade sled for moving goods, a home of "trash, scraps and sod." There are, inescapably, pictures of cemeteries, German and Russian both, or simply a pile of bones he wryly described as "a Russian Soldier on the battlefield in Pripet Swamps, Stokhod River, 1923." And of course, many portraits of the people he met and worked beside, including one of a "peasant teamster" who looks so much like my grandfather himself that I'm never sure whether it is a joke or his twin.

One of the last photos was clearly taken by a different camera, in a different style, perhaps in a professional studio rather than along some village road. It frames a rather dashing young man in a suit jacket with his tie cavalierly swept over one shoulder, his slicked back, collegiate hair and unavoidable front teeth. The caption below reads, "Ilya Tolstoy, 1923." I'd been skimming along when I first saw it, but those words drove me back into the narrative itself to figure out what kind of a Tolstoy this might be and what he was doing in my grandfather's book. Apparently the great Leo's grandson, Ilya, was a member of the Quaker Relief Service's Moscow Office, where he'd already earned a reputation as "competent" before my grandfather's tour of duty for having led a Kirghiz band on a 1,200-mile expedition to Turkestan and beyond to find, purchase, and drive home 1,500 horses. What intrigued my pragmatic ancestor was how, as pacifist Quakers, Ilya and his team had managed to safeguard this valuable live-stock across a country teaming with bandits and militias.

While that might have been a curious side story within the Quaker Relief Service, a sliver of glamor in largely unglamorous work, it took a more personal turn for my grandfather. Just as Ted was heading east to Poland, young Ilya elected to follow the Quaker path west to Penn University; not the one in Philadelphia, but the other Penn University, in Oskaloosa, Iowa, to study agricultural science. One of his classmates, who would become his English tutor, was Ted's younger brother.

Ilya had surely braced himself for a world of provincial hicks, so he must have been quite stunned to learn that his new friend had a brother back on his side of the world. Upon this discovery, Ilya insisted that Ted visit his mother in Moscow, a great honor when the Tolstoys retained unparalleled stature in a world where virtually all hierarchies were in flux. After his assignment in Poland concluded, my grandfather took a long train ride across the Russian plain, which he described in well-informed agricultural detail, to Moscow, but when it comes to that historic meeting, he merely wrote: "Mrs. Tolstoy explained many things to me, and I of course was very appreciative." What those many things were—about the first decade of the Bolshevik reign, of growing up in Leo Tolstoy's home,

the elusive nature of love and the beauty of older women—we will never
know. But blessed by the Tolstoys, Ted was able to travel broadly through
Russia; in two weeks he trained over six thousand miles in Russian third
class and only took his boots off twice. Two very bored secret police tailed
him wherever he went.

Back home in Saline County where he would spend the rest of his life,
Ted founded and then presided over the Missouri Archeological Society,
ultimately publishing five other books, *The Spiro Mound, Tobacco Pipes of
the Missouri Indians, Clay Pipes from Pamplin, Spiro Mound Copper,* and
The Sioux of the Rosebud. When the road crew clearing a new two-lane
highway that would curl underneath my grandfather's hill hit something
strange—a smooth brown fossilized stone—they knew enough about the
old man to call him down. Under his direction they set aside their work on
the road, accepting their new roles of junior archeologists. Over the coming
weeks the crew carefully cleared and cataloged the site, uncovering a large,
nearly complete mastodon skeleton, whose ribs and tusks had been stacked
in a semi-orderly way, suggesting the great beast had been disassembled by
humans. There were also telltale scrapes along the bone, evidence that meat
had been stripped clean by stone tools rather than teeth.

Once labeled, my grandfather had the bones sent to Woods Hole in
Massachusetts for carbon dating, and they came back revealing the beast
was 35,000 years old. "There has to be a mistake," the scientist added. Otherwise these results meant our early ancestors arrived in North America
more than 20,000 years earlier than commonly accepted—a revolution-
izing discovery, and one that corresponded with my grandfather's general
belief that everyone else, and especially those in Ivory Towers, was wrong.
A second test confirmed the first. He wrote a series of papers asserting his
claim, but perhaps because he was too far outside the academy or perhaps
because others could find fault with his methodology or perhaps because of
a general absence of collaborating evidence, his papers went unpublished,
which sparked a nourishing resentment that gave a sense of purpose to his
later years. When the lab that housed these bones mysteriously caught fire,
incinerating the evidence of his discovery, it mostly served to confirm the

conspiracy that had sought to silence him. Two generations later, it sounds like he was right.

My grandfather believed passionately in books, science, and learning while generally seeing The Educated as natural antagonists. It had always been assumed my dad would go to college, but when, given his allergies and hay fever, it also started to become evident he'd never come back, leaving his younger brother to inherit the long days and swollen vertebrae of the farm, my dad became an ambivalent figure within his family, a source of both pride and resentment.

My dad was a good student, and with the elite eastern schools seeking to diversify by adding a few rural kids to their hallowed ranks, he was accepted into one of the most rigorous and self-satisfied. Not surprisingly, he was unprepared to compete, academically or socially, against the well-heeled spawn of Andover or Exeter, and he nearly failed out after a single semester, but Amherst agreed that he could stay on, so long as he was willing to work forty hours a week clearing the tables of his classmates and washing their dishes in the cafeteria.

The obvious path after graduation would have been law or business school, or perhaps a junior job at a New York publishing house, but inspired by his own family's willingness to set out into the world—from the rich farmlands of Missouri to the devastated plains of Poland—and coupled with a sympathy for the provinces, he found instead a job at an English language school in Barranquilla, a port city in the north of Colombia that, in addition to its indigenous roots, had welcomed waves of European immigrants after the wars, as well as Asian and Middle Eastern traders. About the same time my dad was heading south, a young Colombian journalist left Barranquilla to make a pilgrimage to the United States and pay homage to his hero, William Faulkner, traveling across the Southern US by Greyhound. At the end of that trip, Gabriel Garcia Marquez and his wife would settle in Mexico City where he wrote the divine *One Hundred Years of Solitude*.

In the quinine-haze and gin-soaked tradition of ex-pats, my dad spent two years in Barranquilla. He impressed his South American colleagues by casually letting it be known that his dad was the mayor of Miami, a claim affirmed by the impressive seal on the letters he received from home; only some noticed the confusing fine print that specified "Miami, Missouri." He learned Spanish and traveled along the Caribbean coast. For two weeks, he hosted a young, unknown Hunter S. Thompson, who was passing through town as a stringer for American papers and gathering stories that would eventually make it into his novel *The Rum Diaries*. After the first year, he made a quick trip back to the States to claim my mom, who had seduced him in college and whom he now lured south of the border to her parents' horror and her rebellious delight.

By the time they returned, he'd spent the last seven years living among foreigners—first the Blue-Blooded Easterners and then in Colombia. Why stop? With my mom, he went to the University of Virginia, where my sister was born and where he completed a PhD in English with a dissertation on Old English. From there to an associate professor position at Michigan and eventually on to the University of Iowa, which was known for two things, its formidable wrestling team and being home to more embittered, alcoholic writers than anywhere else on earth, thanks to the legendary Iowa Writers Workshop that had been created back in the 1930s as a refuge from the impossibilities of New York. Iowa City was to be a secret place where writers could practice and hone their craft, have sloppy affairs, and ruin their livers. Over the years, a steady flow of greats—Flannery O'Connor, Robert Lowell, John Berryman, Raymond Carver, Donald Justice, Denis Johnson, Jane Smiley, Kurt Vonnegut, Marvin Bell, Rita Dove, Jorie Graham, Michael Cunningham—had made my town their home, and the Workshop continued to be run by high priests and priestesses of literature. Every year a new class of acolytes would appear, full of promise and self-regard. Our papers, not to mention dinner table gossip, would report with great pride when one of "ours" would publish a new book, be reviewed favorably, or otherwise demonstrate how the virtues of being Iowan had in some way elevated them. Although a scholar of Chaucer and Shakespeare, my dad received the departmental perch of editor of *The Iowa Review*, which made him a mentor to many a Workshop student and a gatekeeper to the illusion of literary fame.

As a result, most of my babysitters were aspiring writers—assistant editors from *The Review* and their Workshop pals—and our home was always stacked high with fresh books, half of them by "that guy who was here last month with the Vietnamese girlfriend." We had poets for dinner every Sunday. Most were utterly indifferent to a wide-eyed teenage kid, which was fine as it allowed me to quietly observe their dueling exchanges—John Ashbery: fraud or genius? Stevens or Williams? Which writer would you most like to punch, or bed, or punch and then bed? Who had sold out by turning to scriptwriting and how much had that bastard made? And why—why!—weren't there more readers of serious literature?

Most came and went quickly; a home-cooked meal was nice but they weren't at Iowa to spend their nights with a family. There were always a few, however, who would linger after the others had left for the writers' bars or join us on Christmas Eve when they were alone in town. These were almost always women, and especially those who were not classically, stately beautiful but instead a little off to the side, needing to be discovered; my dad had a gift with them. I remember best the red-haired, freckled Denny with the whistling gap between her teeth; the handsome, equine Sara.

The first two poets I read not as a frustrating school assignment but with pleasure were both gifts from my dad. The first was C.P. Cavafy, an early 20th century Alexandrian Greek. The cover wasn't very promising, with its dirty yellow background as though it had been left in the sun too long or was trying to approximate some feel of yesteryear. But even worse was the large photo of Cavafy himself in a wide lapelled suit with his pocket scarf, staring down at his would-be reader through heavy, round glasses with a look of slight condescension or even annoyance, almost as though we are interrupting him from something far more interesting than our company. The overall effect is a parody of the English gentleman, of a younger man aspiring to be old.

At my dad's encouragement, I forgave the cover and did my best to read a few poems, especially those at the front. One positive quality was that I could understand them, which was generally not the experience I had reading 19th century English poets in school. They were written in a clear, steady voice that wanted to reach its reader rather than lead him on a chase. But more than that, and to my great surprise, what they said was something that I longed to hear: that there was a great journey ahead for me. Cavafy wrote of long roads and distant islands, of dark nights and destinies to fulfill. He wrote about Ithaca, far off on the horizon, and he explained why the Odysseus in me should stop at every port along the way, being in no hurry to reach my destination. "May there be many mornings when," he proposed, a simple mantra that has woven in and out of my life ever since. When he spoke of being a "valiant of voluptuousness," I thought I could be one too. His poems felt like a voice from another age, another world, reaching out to me and welcoming me into adventure. Where it would take me, I couldn't tell, but I knew I was preparing to set out and it was possible that Cavafy could guide the way.

As I read past his early "wise poems" and their promises of adventure, I discovered a second poet, one who spoke in a way, with a quality of emotion, that was quite different from what I had known before. When this Cavafy wrote about unnamed men, gods, or minor characters plucked from the history of ancient Greece and Byzantium, he did so with affection for the elements that made us most human rather than most heroic. His sympathy was always with those who made bad decisions justified by their sensual desires rather than in illusory pursuit of momentary power. As only a provincial can, he wrote slightly askew to main currents of the past, giving voice to the side characters, the bit players. For Cavafy, many of those most enduring moments were times of unabashed gay desire, two young men in a squalid hotel as it is the only place that will shelter them. I felt quite sophisticated reading those poems, but also perhaps a little bit unsure when about this same time my mother gave me a copy of *Keep the River on Your Right*, Tobias Schneebaum's memoir of living among a Stone Age tribe in the Amazon, an adventure of self-discovery and homoeroticism among the natives. She assured me I'd love it.

The other poet my dad introduced me to was Jack Gilbert, whose second book, *Monolithos*, was still in hardback then. Unlike Cavafy's, this one looked like poetry: the cover was framed by two large rectangles; I suppose

those are monoliths? The outer one all specked grey; the inner descending
from shear blackness to a kind of dawn. It was thin, the kind of book that
could survive a long journey. Everything about this book said there was
something important inside it. And it didn't disappoint. The poems have
a powerful directness, and Gilbert's constant themes about lust, about the
vast appetites of the body, hungers in himself he both adores and works to
master, were ones I was beginning to understand all too well.

And then one night Gilbert himself was in our house after a local
reading he'd given, followed back by a gaggle of English professors and
Workshop poets. He was silver haired and lupine, and when he spoke,
softly, the whole room (but especially the women half his age) was held in
rapt attention. He talked about his childhood among the empty steel mills
of Pittsburgh, about his days riding Greyhound buses across the country,
about making love on a cold stone floor. He (who published two books in
his first sixty years) talked about challenging himself to write one hundred
poems in one hundred days. But he also asked questions—never to the
room as a whole, but always singling out a person, giving them all of his
frightful attention. What did they expect writing to give them? Were they
interested in what they knew or in what they didn't know?

I had been gratefully anonymous, with all eyes focused on Gilbert
or his rotating interviewee, when suddenly he turned to me, bringing the
whole room with him, and asked, "Colin, why do you want to be a poet?"

After a moment of stunned silence—stunned that he'd seen this in me
at a glance, stunned that he remembered my name, stunned that I had no
answer—he tried to rescue me. Was it, he prompted, out of a compulsive
need to relive and make sense of my experiences? Was it out of a secret
infatuation with my own voice, a motive he graciously, revealingly, implied
was not all bad. Did I romanticize a life of poverty and neglect? Did I have
something I needed to say?

All of those things were true, but each a fraction of the truth, splinters
that could never be assembled into a whole. The silence was swollen and
horrible; I could feel the embarrassment of some, the annoyance of others,
especially the men, that this kid had somehow stolen the focus of their

party, and suddenly I—desperate to say something, anything—mumbled out, "I think it's probably because I'm from Iowa City." And with that the room burst into laughter.

But not Gilbert, who just smiled and held me in his steely gaze. I think he understood completely that while we did many of the same things kids everywhere else did—ride our bikes to the pool, play Dungeons & Dragons, collect aluminum cans from garbage bins for the five-cent refund and in so doing occasionally stumble across stacks of discarded, mind-altering gay pornography, take odd jobs delivering papers and washing dishes—there was a different hierarchy here, where money and power were looked on with a certain disdain, where we felt a kind of pity for the empty lives of doctors and lawyers, and in this peculiar inversion of reality the greatest achievement imaginable wasn't to walk on the moon or command an army but to become immortal through words alone.

THE CINNAMON SHOPS

I was straining to make sense of what was being said. The coal-eyed poet spoke in a near whisper from the front of the room, the upper level of a bookstore packed with university students, faculty, and townspeople, her voice mirroring the ethereal qualities of her verse, ghost lines and half-formed thoughts that suggested some immense secret just beyond our uninitiated grasp. But try as I might, her words kept slipping by me and my attention waned. She had thick, stylishly unkempt hair and her lower arms were be-ringed by silver bracelets. Reading glasses perched low on her long nose, and her eyes would often rise above them to hold us in her reverent gaze as she continued to intone. I felt Andrzej lean toward me, his floral cologne arriving first, and he said, not especially quietly but in the most refined of foreign accents, "Isn't she the type you'd like to slap around while fucking?" People in several directions fidgeted and I turned a criminal shade of red.

During that uncertain period of my life, older men had a disconcert-ing habit of telling me their sexual fantasies. In addition to Andrzej, there was Jim North, for example, our ex-marine next-door neighbor who could be seen each bright morning jogging by with a pair of iron barbells in his gigantic, knuckled fists. At one boozy backyard barbeque, he wrapped me in his sweaty arm and whispered sloppily, "Kid, if I ever get divorced and you need to find me, I'll be in Helsinki. Jesus, the women. They're so beau-tiful. They don't even wear bras and they proposition you on the street!" Taking me by the shoulders and staring deeply into my soul, he made certain I understood: "*They* proposition *you*. On the *street*. Oh my god," he said wiping a lone tear from his muscular cheek, "The tits!"

Not to mention my own dad, though his usually slipped out by accident and my bad habit of occasionally reading his mail.

During my adolescence, the Kuchars, a pair of Polish neurologists who had been misplaced in Iowa, were my parents' closest friends. Andrzej was short with a dramatic coif of hair, a sharply pointed nose and a smart, perverse grin. Through years of running a lab together, they'd settled into their roles, and Hanna was happy to go about the work of scanning brains and analyzing data while he waved his arms about and sparkled. She did her best to be overlooked, dressing in dark, loose linens that gave no particular clue, and happily allowing her hair to become prematurely streaked with grey. Her smile revealed imperfect, continental teeth. You could pass her on the street or see her at dinner a dozen times without realizing how beautiful she was, until you saw it and it became inescapable. Outside of the lab, she was an amateur sculptor, crafting small bronze figures that invariably ended up mounting our dining room table—a heavily breasted nude cut from the mid-thighs up; a cat with one leg sticking straight out, licking its swollen crotch; two lithe, naked and encoiled youth.

One summer they gave me a job working in their lab, which was so unlike my dad's English Department where I'd roamed the dark halls for years but where no one had ever offered to pay me. Everything here, where they believed that some truths actually exist and that it would be a good thing to know them, was brightly lit and orderly, with professors directing post-graduates supervising graduate students commanding undergraduates and somewhere beneath them, me. Every surface was clean and bare. I was assigned data entry and simple administrative tasks, but eventually someone had mercy and I was allowed to help prepare various tests to locate and measure types of brain damage, generally brought on by strokes, such as a facial recognition inventory where subjects were challenged to recognize utterly expressionless photographs of famous people, or another exam where blindfolded subjects were asked to identify small objects we placed in either their right or left hands—a plastic lion, a key, a thick rubber band, a bottle cap.

Andrzej loved to tell stories about Phineas Gage, one of the great case studies in brain science. While working on a railroad, an explosion drove an iron rod through Gage's skull—or more precisely, through his left frontal lobe. To everyone's surprise, he survived, or at least someone did. What family and friends all reported was that the person they'd known was replaced by another, a violent man with a short fuse, easily flustered. In the world of the neurology lab, the reality that we were someone today was no guarantee that tomorrow or the day after an iron rod or a little bolt of electricity might rattle our brains and release someone new, and almost always someone worse.

While the Kuchars had not found their Gage yet, they were assembling a menagerie of bizarre cases. Stroke victims who'd lost not just a sense of smell but their ability to use nouns, even while adjectives and verbs remained intact. A farmer who was convinced he was blind although he responded to visual stimuli. I was particularly haunted by a man in his late 40s perhaps because his ailment was not linked to a stroke, which as an adolescent I knew I'd never have, but by syphilis, which, though a virgin, seemed inevitable if things worked out as I hoped. The disease had gone to his brain and wiped it virtually clear, so that his memory had been reduced to a forty-five-second span. If you left the room and returned a minute later, he'd have no idea he'd ever met you before. There are all kinds of versions of hell, but his particular torment was an obsessive concern with smoking, peeing, and masturbating—three simple acts, including two that concerned me deeply, that he knew he needed to perform every so often, and which he was unable to remember when he'd done them last, thus casting him into a perpetual suspicion that it was time.

"Time is the thing that keeps everything from happening at once," Andrzej explained to me. "Because this patient had lost his memory, and therefore control of time, everything is pressing upon him in a single, overwhelming present." That seemed very profound to me then, and even years later when I realized Andrzej had cribbed the best part from a science fiction writer.

I was still reading Cavafy and Gilbert, but the writers I knew best were the wholly male American trinity of Mark Twain, Hemingway, and

F. Scott Fitzgerald. Faulkner was a bit too obscure, his South too impenetrable. Branching out, barely, I had gulped down Raymond Carver, so clean and perfect. I found Paul Auster's *New York Trilogy* and Jay McInerney's *Bright Lights, Big City* on my own, but mostly it was my dad who nudged me into more playful territory with finds like Robert Coover's *The Universal Baseball Association, Inc., J. Henry Waugh, Prop.*, which shared my own obsessions with baseball statistics and simulation games, and then the revelation, *One Hundred Years of Solitude*. Suddenly other books from around the world, like Salman Rushdie's *Midnight's Children*, Milan Kundera's *The Unbearable Lightness of Being*, and Yukio Mishima's *The Sound of Waves* were beginning to infiltrate my shelves. And then the notion of reading anything that wasn't from far away started to feel like a waste; the books I wanted were beacons that somehow signaled how far the world stretched out beyond my grasp, books that in some way could light my path out into something stranger. That's where I was going.

For my seventeenth birthday, Andrzej and Hanna gave me a copy of Bruno Schulz's *The Cinnamon Shops*. Just holding it I felt a little older. And then I opened it. Schulz was a thicket—long, knotty sentences, unexpected twists, shadows and ambiguities—but rather than lock me out, it was as though the narrowest of doors had opened and once I stepped through, they pulled shut behind me, locking me in a world utterly different—more alluring, more nourishingly deviant—from anything I'd known before.

He wrote about his hometown of Drohobycz, a kind of Yoknapatawpha County or Macondo, inbred and circular, lost to the rest of the world, with a veneer of innocence that just thinly covers its own decay and perversity. Schulz's adventures are always told from a child's point of view, naïve and filled with wonder, but it is a child constantly discovering a world of dangers and temptations, a world where everything is in constant flux, with people changing into bugs or even—in his uncle's case—an enema tube. One spring day he stumbles upon a half-wit girl "hoarse with shaking, convulsed with madness," masturbating herself against a tree. In time he learns telltale signs of a schoolgirl's future corruption and how to detect menstruating girls by the way they blush. Schulz peels back the scrim of normality to reveal hidden streets and listen in on odious philosophies, but his stories never behave as stories should, progressing from one point through some arc to another, but rather twist their way to some end that often seems entirely disconnected from where they'd begun, ending because they'd exhausted themselves rather than because they'd reached any destination.

Balancing Schulz's naïve child is the demented patriarch, his father, who holds the family and the household staff captive while he lectures on about the secret lives of tailor's dummies or strange dreams of transformation. Obsessed with harnessing the power of creation for himself, this father collects and cross breeds exotic birds, creating a monstrous aviary and almost succeeding in taking flight himself. But for all his power, Father is easily controlled by the family's wicked, ripe maid who—simply by pointing her finger and threatening to tickle the old man—can drive him trembling from the room.

Though I'd begun to suspect its existence, it was Schulz who taught me about the thirteenth month, that grotesque and fertile time when his stories began. "Everybody knows that in a run of normal uneventful years that great eccentric, Time, begets sometimes other years, different, prodigal years which—like a sixth, smallest toe—grow a thirteenth freak month." At any normal time, a young boy could dart home from the theater to retrieve his father's wallet and it would be a simple, safe task. But during the thirteenth month, there is a great risk in sending a boy out on such an errand, where he might become lost in unexpected streets, behind doors that didn't exist the day before. On such a night, an innocent youth may be "touched by the divine finger of poetry."

When I told Andrzej how much I loved Schulz's book, he answered that it was a miracle the stories exist at all. As a young man, he shared, Schulz had almost made it out of Drohobycz and into another destiny altogether. A Polish-speaking Jew, born in the dying days of the Hapsburg Empire, Schulz had been a star student at the local high school, but his frail health and social awkwardness made his two attempts to escape by university, first at the Lviv Polytechnic then again in Vienna to study architecture, a failure. Healthy or sick, home or away, Schulz was constantly drawing—heavy black and white expressionist illustrations. His most recurring image is a long-legged, regal woman lording indifferently over a pile of huddled, groveling men. You can often find Schulz among them, his jug-handle ears framing his oversized head and pointy nose, looking like a child in a man's suit and top hat.

The greater world wasn't for Schulz, and ultimately the same high school headmaster who had ushered him out into it allowed him back as an unlicensed, and thus further underpaid, high school art instructor. A shy, haunted presence, Schulz would confuse his students with fairy tale-like lectures about the pencil in his hand and its perfectly understandable dream of returning to the forest, where it would grow to become the grandest of oaks, home to a hundred crows as black as the graphite in its soul. Can you imagine, he asked them, the pencil's confusion as he transformed it instead, stroke by stroke, line by line, before their eyes into a shop merchant with high-arching, Old Testament eyebrows, towering over a mound of linens and bedding? Or he might begin a lesson by addressing the stepsisterly resentment of the easel, always destined to hold the perfect, white canvas that so mesmerizes the artist, who attentively, lovingly brushes its façade with golds and reds. Oh, how the easel cried, if only someday the prince would notice her! How steady she is, how true! Everything in Schulz's classroom—a jug of water, the window shade, the blackboard, the students' most secret thoughts—felt perilously close to life.

It was, then as now, hardly a living, and when his merchant father died and Bruno lacked all aptitude or desire to take over the business, his family's fortune went into steady decline. By the time he met Wladyslaw Riff while recuperating at a resort high in the Tatra Mountains, Schulz was in his early thirties, a college dropout, unmarried and unpromising. Ten years his junior, Riff was handsome and outgoing, even though his youthful vitality was withering away with consumption, but the two lonely men discovered they shared a love of literature and a desire to write.

Not long after Schulz's return to Drohobycz, he received a letter from Riff. Schulz felt so grateful to the envelope that he dreaded tearing it. In his eventual reply, he explained this fear to Riff, and how he was only able to open the envelope by turning this scene into a holy sacrifice of sorts. With a silent prayer, his penknife slit its belly and a letter was offered up. These letters began the conversation Schulz had been waiting to have all his life—about the mystery of books, the stories constantly echoing inside himself in fragments and images, about his attempts to make some sense of it all. Schulz and Riff wrote each other constantly, saying the things that only friends can say, and giving one another the confidence to believe that their own peculiar takes on reality might be of interest to anyone beside themselves. But within a year, Riff had succumbed to tuberculosis. Out of fear of the disease, his family had all of his papers—the poems, a novel manuscript, and his letters—burned.

With Riff's death, the stories that were beginning to take shape within Schulz atrophied. He could only tell his stories to someone else, and there was no one listening. Still, one summer a local chemistry professor arranged for an exhibition of Schulz's drawings at a gallery a nearby town known mostly as a health resort. As victories go, it was decidedly minor, and yet any artist who has been denied publication or gallery shows could imagine Schulz's exhilaration and terror.

As it happened, a legendary eighty-year-old Polish senator on one of his nurse-aided ambles wandered into the exhibit. In a kinder story, he would praise Schulz to the stars, then carry him on his broad if aged shoulders to Warsaw for a champagne toast. But in fact he denounced Schulz's work as hideous pornography and demanded the show be shut down. As in some 1920s silent movie where the Little Men outmaneuver the Boss while bumping heads and falling over a few times, Schulz and the gallery owner agreed, yes, yes, this horrible offense must be taken down, and went to work moving pieces from one wall to another until the Senator was recalled to the capitol and the exhibit could resume. Nearly every piece sold, perhaps thanks to the Senator's unintended promotion and Schulz's timidity in pricing.

Through a shared acquaintance, Schulz was introduced to Debora Vogel, a poet and admirer of modern art who lived in a neighboring town.

Surely they were paired as a man and a woman with mutual artistic sensibilities and the common absence of a spouse. And they found some affinity, cultivated over walks and coffees, but it was only when they returned to their respective homes and began to exchange letters that they were able to reach a kind of intimacy. Encouraged by Vogel, Schulz filled letter after letter with extraordinary stories about his family and their fellow Drohobycz residents.

In a postscript to one in which Schulz had described a lone hero lost in a fathomless city, he asked Debora if she would marry him. It's easy to understand why her parents would be wary of an odd, middle-aged art teacher from a family in decline, but Debora had doubts of her own. Throughout his stories, Schulz continually returned to the mutability of matter. "Reality takes on certain shapes merely for the sake of appearance, as a joke or form of play," he wrote. "One person is a human, another is a cockroach, but the shape does not penetrate essence, is only a role adopted for the moment, an outer skin soon to be shed... the migration of forms is the essence of life." How would she give her life to a man who constantly warned that he could become something else entirely?

Perhaps out of some lingering guilt, or maybe simply because she loved them, Debora arranged Schulz's stories and shared them with a journalist she knew, who agreed that he'd never read anything quite like them. Through the journalist, the stories reached an esteemed writer and editor who must have dreaded the package. How many of these had been pushed upon her by the mothers, lovers, and children of unacknowledged genius? But she also fell under their spell.

Soon after *The Cinnamon Shops* was in print it became an improbable literary sensation, the talk of salons in Warsaw and Cracow. Awards and prizes followed, including the Golden Laurel from the Polish Academy of Literature, welcoming Schulz into an exclusive world of the Polish artistic elite. But while *The Cinnamon Shops* was still in production, Bruno learned that Debora had married an architect from Lviv. Their correspondence stopped.

As a newly anointed Great Writer, other correspondences began, but they were marked by a different formality. He was invited to publish in various Polish and German magazines, but he had lost his voice. In a world where everyone else seemed to be charging into the future, Schulz continued to wander aimlessly through the same streets and shops that had circumscribed his life. He published a second book, *Sanatorium Under the Sign of the Hourglass*, mostly composed of earlier stories that never made it into *The Cinnamon Shops*, stories with glimmers of weird genius but lesser effect. Beyond that, there are many references to a magnum opus, *The Messiah*, the epic novel he either wrote or more likely dreamed of writing, but no manuscript pages have ever been found. Perhaps they were magnificent.

Drohobycz was shaken from its timelessness in 1939, dragged into consciousness by the arrival of the Soviet army, and suddenly his world transformed into something entirely different. Schulz tried and failed to write for those dialectical materialists, whose theory of relentless, inevitable change was so different than his chaotic vision of the mutability of matter. A few years later, the town was overrun by German troops, who began to star Jews and drive them into ghettos.

The Nazis attracted any number of mid-level officers and even high command who fancied themselves connoisseurs and patrons of the arts, and one—Felix Landau, a cabinet maker who told people he was an architect—took Schulz under his dubious protection, paying him with loaves of bread, the odd cabbage or sack of beans, occasionally an invitation to what must have been a truly terrifying dinner, in exchange for a portrait first of himself and then of his horse, and ultimately frescos for the Gestapo headquarters. These and other odd jobs for Landau sustained Schulz and his surviving family for months, even as the Nazis murdered their friends and neighbors.

Just as certain forces seek to annihilate, there are other, sometimes balancing forces that lift the caterpillar from the road. In the genocidal Nazi occupation of Poland, resistance fighters helped disrupt supply lines to the East. They passed intelligence—maps, sketches and reports—to the government in exile and the British military. Some helped smuggle children out of the Jewish ghetto in Warsaw. They stockpiled weapons. A few at least, and maybe more, read literature.

One of those was Jerzy Ficowski, a member of the Polish Home Army. As an eighteen-year-old in 1942, he was given a copy of *The Cinnamon Shops* by a friend, which he read knowing that any day he could be arrested or see his family and friends killed. In its pages he discovered what he recognized as the greatest writer of his time. In the middle of a war zone, he tracked down Schulz's address and wrote him a gushing letter expressing his vast gratitude for Bruno's work, and the humblest of hopes that Schulz might reply. He never did, sadly. Who knows what he might have said? Although Schulz was still alive, he'd lost his home and it is unclear, perhaps unlikely, if Ficowski's letter ever reached him. Within a few months, he was shot dead in the street by a rival Gestapo officer, who celebrated having killed "Landau's Jew."

In the war's final years, Schulz' town was destroyed, and virtually all of his correspondents died, their homes pillaged and burnt. His readers were scattered or dead. After the war, the world wasn't much kinder to him. As a Jew and Polish-language writer, he was of no interest to the Ukrainian authorities that liberated and claimed Drohobycz. As a decadent fabulist, he had no place in the Soviet realist canon. But Ficowski kept his copy of *The Cinnamon Shops* though he lost almost everything else, and after the war, he gathered what letters and illustrations could be saved, ultimately publishing the first biography of Schulz, and fighting to bring his books back to print. Although Schulz was lost to a full generation, by the early 1980s his works were filling Solidarity-era Polish bookstores and soon after translations into German, English, French, and Italian, and at least a dozen other languages followed. And a few years later, a copy was given to me at that exact moment when I was ready for a very different kind of story.

Part Two

REASONS FOR MOVING

As someone with a limited loyalty to the truth, I'm often content to tell others what they want to hear if it will make my life easier, so I surprised myself by responding so bluntly, so honestly to the man who had fallen into step with me on the sidewalk in Dar es Salaam. The first part happened to me there repeatedly: I'd be walking along, wondering why the street smelled like a burning tire, hoping I didn't accidentally make eye contact with a beggar whose legs had been twisted by polio and whose eyes saw straight into my privileged soul, when a stranger would amble up beside me and try to start a conversation by asking if I spoke English or where I was from. This time it was a man who could have stuffed me comfortably inside himself and then eaten a large meal. He asked proudly what I thought about his city. "A filthy dump," I replied. Although I desperately wanted to believe just the opposite, to claim I had discovered some secret charm within Dar es Salaam, this truth was just too overwhelming to deny. I started to peel away from him by crossing the street.

I assumed that would be that, but I felt him stop behind me, felt his anger simmering—as though it were some physical thing that could reach me across the street and smack me. "Are you always so rude?" he asked, raising his voice so I couldn't escape it, so that the whole street heard his threat. No, I thought, not always. In fact, I'm generally just the opposite: the kind of young man whom girlfriends' parents are relieved to meet. But it had already been a very bad week and perhaps I wasn't quite who I thought I had been.

"And your name," he added, "Colin Hamilton, isn't it?"

Is there a single thing he could have said that would have surprised me more? I was an anonymous traveler in a city of strangers. No one knew who I was, where I was, why I was there. But this man knew my name, and I felt all my clocks freeze. I turned around and he was waiting for me with a scrap of paper in his hand, radiating pride in the power he'd just exhibited. "Colin Hamilton?" he cooed with brutal satisfaction, "and I think you wrote this?" It was my name and address, in my own writing. "Yes," he confirmed, "I think you did." Four days before I hadn't been so rude, to my current regret and perhaps explaining my current behavior.

In fact, I'd been desperately lonely, which made me vulnerable and polite. So then when a college student had asked if I'd join him for a chai, that smoky, ubiquitous Tanzanian drink with the faint taste of goat udder, after an innocent enough introduction on a crowded bus, I agreed. Almost immediately I knew I'd made a mistake. If I thought I'd get some comfort from the generic exchanges of foreignness, that I could pretend I'd made a friend or earned a story I could tell back at home, I was wrong. This was not going to be a happy cultural exchange. He was thin and clean shaven in a worn white shirt. What I took at first as a glimmer of curiosity in his moist eyes sharpened into something else, a little tool. He wrapped up the small talk and drove to his point as the chai arrived. He was, he assured me, more than he seemed. (So am I, I thought, so am I!) He was a South African activist who had found temporary refuge from Apartheid in Tanzania, but now his visa was up and he could be deported at any time to certain arrest and torture at home.

"You could help me," he added.

He told me how. He needed money to buy his way out of it—with just $50 American dollars, he could get a visa extension. That $50 might be the difference between his life and death, he told me. Reflexively, I said I couldn't help. I told him I was a student myself, on a small fellowship, and had barely enough to get me through this trip. It was true, in a way, at least from my perspective, but he continued to push. Surely I could spare something? Twenty dollars? Five? Could I sit across the table from him, knowing the danger he faced—torture, maybe death—and do nothing? What was his life, a human life, worth to me?

Although I felt guilty, the more he pushed, the more rigid I became, the more resolute in refusal. But for some reason, I lacked the nerve to do the obvious—stand up, slap down a few coins for the chai and walk out, which would be to call his bluff, to clarify that no matter what I could or couldn't do, I was unmoved by his lie. Something held me back. He was lying, of course, but I knew that I was too—a student yes, but for weeks I'd been pretending to be a researcher, a student anthropologist, which felt so much more meaningful than being a mere tourist or even traveler, pretending to have some understanding let alone command of where I was, pretending that I couldn't spare a few bucks to help some guy who almost certainly had never even been to South Africa but was, convincingly, desperate. We were both lying, and we continued in an unsteady truce, each wanting to expose the other without revealing our self.

"No," I said, "I really can't," trying to stay firm, but also aware of my own wobble.

To my relief, he changed his approach. If I couldn't give him a single dollar, would I at least give him my address in America? He was applying for a visa, and if he could demonstrate that he had friends in the States who could help him, it was more likely to be granted. "It won't cost you a thing," he added, knowing that would reassure and insult me. It seemed like the fastest way out, at least without creating a scene, so I said sure. He pulled a scrap of paper and pencil stub from his pocket and pushed them across the table to me.

* * *

"Your friend, the South African terrorist," the man, "is in our custody. And I have orders to bring you in." Then he flashed me something silver strapped to his belt that could have been a police badge. "Let's go." Like an impatient adult taking a child by the wrist, he encircled my sparrow bicep with his hand and steered me into his city.

I'd been in and out of Dar es Salaam over the past two weeks and had spent time there the summer before. I took an arrogant pride in how well I knew my way around; on the list of things that made me me, that would have shown up somewhere as a way for a kid from Iowa to keep even with his new New York college friends. But it turns out I didn't know the alleys; he did. He moved me down one, another, and within minutes all my straight lines had been irreparably bent. It had as much to do with being out of place as being in a complete mental meltdown. There was a glitch in my brain that couldn't get past the simple "he shouldn't know my name," which kept repeating itself in a numbing loop, to more pressing issues, like, "what do I do?"

Unable to think for myself, I listened as he explained the facts quickly, not bothering to wait for answers I couldn't possibly give: a vile terrorist plot had been uncovered, and my name and address had been found on the chief perpetrator. Why would I know a South African terrorist if we weren't collaborators? Was I his money man? His connection to arms dealers? There were orders to arrest me. I'd be brought before a judge for questioning tomorrow or the next day, perhaps next week. Until then, I'd be stuck in a Tanzanian jail, which, he assured me in case I had any illusions, was a very ugly place.

I wanted to say I was none of those things. Just an American, a dumb American admittedly. I wanted to say I'm here doing research, as though that might justify me or even interest him—who wouldn't want to be the subject of my studies? But I was just lucid enough to remember there is such a thing as a research visa and I'd never gotten one.

"Listen," he said, as though he were interrupting me, as though I'd managed to get out a single word. "Listen, you don't seem like such a bad kid." He looked me up and down to confirm his assessment; it was the impression I gave off. "Maybe there has been a mistake? Maybe the judge is mistaken. Do you want to talk about it?"

"Yes. Yes, this doesn't make any sense."

"No, it doesn't," he agreed, with a kind of tired resignation. "But I have my orders. Still, let's have a drink before this gets out of control."

He'd stopped us in front of a bar, a bit of a dive or maybe just what a Dar es Salaam bar with no pretense of serving tourists looks like: concrete floors, dated, faded soccer posters and others celebrating the exotic charms of Zanzibar and Harare. The smell of roasted goat and beer. A plywood board bar painted aqua blue. Even on this hot day, the bar had the radiant chill of shaded concrete. There were a few people here and there, mostly sitting in twos, but he steered me to a booth near the back where four men were waiting. "My colleagues," he said by way of introductions and two of them rose so I could sit in the corner, with the five of them looking back at me, a little antelope wondering how he might possibly feed an entire pack of lions. I realized I had done my best not to look at this man on the street, and once he'd seized me, we'd walked side by side; it was only now that I could see him, though I instinctively felt my eyes drop from his watery gaze. I could, however, see his mouth, how it curled down to the right, not cruelly but with a kind of tired inevitability; he wasn't reveling in his power but seemed rather bored by it, as if he already knew everything that would happen next, as if he'd been through this routine too many times. When the waitress came, he ordered a round of Tuskers. I wasn't used to drinking at eleven in the morning, but I also wasn't used to being abducted, if that's what this was, by the police, if that's who they were.

I felt a shimmer of relief run through me with the beer, the shock of the cold, bubbling brew like a little electrical charge re-igniting my brain. Not that I was safe, but my mind was finally catching up with events, and I began to understand what was happening. I was being robbed, not arrested. I almost wanted to smile with self-disgust that it had taken me this long to figure that out. Not a good thing, not in the least, but almost certainly better than being deposited in a Tanzanian jail for the night. And I suppose, I thought, I should take comfort in the fact that they were making the effort to con me rather than just shaking me free of a couple teeth and whatever dollars I had. Then I realized: that's because they know I'm worth more than the cash I had on me.

* * *

I'd arrived at college assuming I would study literature as it was the most noble of pursuits and something of a birthright. It was, therefore, destabilizing when I found myself stumbling through courses on the metaphysical poets or *Ulysses*. How could all my fellow students, these tragically unpoetic people, write so capably about rhyme and meter, about symbolism, about irony, and why did all the questions we were asked leave me so cold and clueless?

What did make sense was anthropology, and as soon as I could I wormed my way out of the sterile, naval gazing English Department and into the grand adventure of Otherness. I told myself that if I was preparing myself to write, wasn't the most apt study learning to observe, to appreciate difference, to loosen one's mind into other realities? With the help of a professor I spent a summer on exchange with a dozen students from across the US in northern Tanzania. Though I'm certain we did nothing of genuine use on our mission, it had awoken within me a new possibility of self that was further inflamed by reading Bruce Chatwin, the poetic wanderer whose xenomania has since gone out of vogue but who once was a kind of hero, at least to those of us anchored in comfort but hungering for a different way of being in the big world. With the help of the same professor, I marked out a plan for return the following summer and even secured a small grant to conduct research for a senior thesis on the relationship between tourism and cultural development, which could very well put me on a path to a PhD program. I could see a life taking shape that was in every way the opposite of the depressing story of settling down, losing vitality, making compromises. I'd become an anthropologist and spend half my time in some foreign world—maybe Tanzania but more likely I'd go deeper, where my imagined rivals couldn't follow—where I'd learn the language, make friends, become a curious part of the community, and almost certainly have primitive, erotic experiences I'd have to leave out of my academic books, with the other half at a prestigious university writing and lecturing. And of course, in my spare time I could churn out a novel or two grounded in my suddenly worldly perspective and experiences.

The second summer I arrived back in Dar es Salaam full of bluster, and so pleased to be able to distinguish myself, even if only in the comfort of my mind, from the hoards of young westerners who were simply traveling while I was *researching*. But what did that actually mean? Was I supposed to walk up to tourists and ask them if they were so naïve that they imagined

what they saw bore any correspondence to actual reality? Was I supposed
to ask a Tanzanian if he felt like he was performing whenever a westerner
was near? Was I supposed to sit back and observe? Nervously I filled my
notebook, but mostly about myself—how alone I felt, how outside the easy
flow of strangers. I felt the immensity of impending failure, knowing that
before long I'd be heading back to college having learned nothing, having
to account for this opportunity I'd been given and squandered. But I also
suspected that if I could have a single meaningful experience—make a
friend, understand an essential truth, see Tanzania even for a moment as
it really was—I might still be redeemed, which surely explained why I had
been willing to accept a simple invitation to chai.

* * *

In sympathy with how slowly my brain was processing this turn of events,
the man explained again: they'd broken up a terrorist plot and among the
incriminating evidence they gathered, they'd found my name and address,
in my own handwriting it appeared, on the chief perpetrator, who'd given
me up under interrogation. Guilty or not, there were difficult questions
that needed to be answered, and he and his men were under orders to arrest
me. In Tanzania, justice was both hard and slow. I'd probably sit in jail at
least overnight and maybe several weeks before the judge could question
me. Surely then I could sort things out, but between now and then…well,
I was going to see more of Tanzania than I'd bargained for.

"But we are not bad men," he assured me, "and I don't believe you are
either," two phrases I wanted very much to believe. "If there were some way
that we could help, some way to convince the judge that you are just a young
American on holiday. In this country, you know, there are always ways to
solve a problem, if you have friends to help you. Do you need a friend now?
Perhaps I could go to the judge on your behalf and make all this go away?"

I must have lit up like a little puppy, but then he added more sternly,
"Let me see your declaration form."

The Tanzanian Shilling was artificially inflated, creating an active
black market for exchange. To protect against this, all foreigners needed

to declare the funds they brought into the country, and every time we legally exchanged currency, that transaction was recorded on an official form. When you left the country, you showed the document, and if, for example, you spent two months in Tanzania while only legally exchanging a hundred dollars, you might have some explaining to do. The other thing the declaration form did, which mattered most in this particular instance, was tell him exactly how much money I had brought into his country. Not knowing what else I could do, I handed it over.

He studied it for a moment, nodding and calculating. Even before he got the words out, I knew what his price would be: half of everything I had. Yes, he was pretty sure that for $500 the judge would dismiss my case outright, and I could go on my merry way, even on a safari, he gamely suggested. Although I knew it was coming, as soon as I heard the number my mind contracted, bracing for the ruin that debt would cause. But what was that ruin, really, I continued to think? Not The End, but something that would force me into a humiliating call home. If I was willing to confess to my parents what a fool I'd been, there would be help. Still, I felt a kind of calm come over me when he finally said it; everything was starting to make sense, to fall into form with roles that I could play. I was not under arrest. I was being robbed. I was not being violently mugged. I was being conned. He said $500, but it was trial and I was supposed to negotiate.

"There is no way I could do that," I said, after evidently doing some math in my head and surely looking convincingly distraught. "I'm here another six weeks."

"Your family could send more," he suggested helpfully.

"No, they couldn't," I lied. "My father's dead, he died when I was young. And my mom, she's sick. I'm only here on a student scholarship. This is it. This is all I have."

He nodded, considering his options. I couldn't tell what he believed. "How much is possible?" he asked.

And while I still felt scared, I was finally beginning to also feel angry, which is one of the hardest emotions for me, but also one I needed right then.

"$50," I said remembering the first man's original price, "I think I could do $50."

I expected him to react dramatically, to feign insult and to threaten. That he didn't told me everything would be okay if I didn't screw up again. It was just a negotiation and the borders had been set. If we all stuck to our roles, I wasn't going to get beaten up and they were going to get something worthwhile for their troubles. Maybe this is what happens, I thought in a moment of anthropological clarity, when subjects decide they don't want to be studied? After some back and forth, we eventually settled on $125.

The hitch, however, was that I didn't have $125 in cash. I had maybe half that; the rest was locked up in traveler's checks that only I could cash. We agreed we'd go to a bank together. They'd wait outside. I'd go in, exchange the checks. Then I'd pay up and we'd be done with each other. Assuming, he reminded me, that the judge agreed $125 was enough.

Though he'd managed to completely disorient me on our way to this bar, I was surprised by how quickly, in just a block or so, we were back on streets I knew, and there everything was the same: Tanzanians on their way to or from work, school, lunch. And lots and lots of apparent mes— Americans, Brits, Australians, Germans—going about the business of seeing the world, of polishing their shiny selves. He tried at first to make some friendly small talk—what had I seen while in Tanzania? Mt. Kilimanjaro? The Serengeti National Park? He always recommended Lake Victoria to tourists, he added. But what little pride I had left allowed me to keep silent, and he gave me that.

At the Barclay's, they left me at the door as promised and I entered another world—quiet, orderly, scentless. I got in line and thought about what to do. There was a security guard near the door. He looked tired, uninspired. If I told him what was happening, would he make it his business to help? Hard to say. And what exactly was happening? The mystery remained whether they were actually cops—bad cops clearly, but possibly that. I thought about calling the American Embassy for help, but right then I had the depressing realization that I'd rather just part with $125 than either have to fess up about how I'd been so easily conned or risk re-escalating a problem that was ready to be solved. Outside, with staged discretion that fooled no one as no one was bothering to watch, I handed over the money and he counted it twice.

"I think the judge will be satisfied," he assured me.

"I'm sure he will," I replied, trying to sound tough or proud or whatever I could muster. He held out his hand until I submitted and shook it, his strong grip fully encompassing my own, a final reminder of what it meant to be in his grasp, and we went our separate ways.

In all likelihood they were thrilled with their take, and they'd happily disappear back into whatever world they'd emerged from. But there was a possibility that they were about to begin an incredible bender and that by around midnight, after hours of telling each other over and over again how easy I'd been, how terrified I looked, they'd have burnt through my money and decided that perhaps it hadn't been enough to dissuade the judge after all. The biggest mystery to me was how they had found me, days after that first meeting, but if they'd done it once, undoubtedly they could do it again.

I went back to my hotel, shoved everything I had into my backpack and checked out. At the port, I bought a ticket on the overnight ferry to Mombasa, a town several hours north and over the Kenyan border. I had no illusion that I'd be able to do any of my "research" there, but hopefully I could just melt on a beach until I'd regained my bearings.

The downside to my escape route was that the ferry didn't leave for five hours, and there was absolutely no place in Dar es Salaam where I wanted to be for even another second. I desperately wanted to become invisible but at the station I felt spot lit on a stage, the one person who looked like he might start crying at any moment surrounded by packs of smug travelers chumming it up and swapping tales of self-building adventure. I walked out the door and into an area of town I hardly knew. A few blocks later I was standing on a corner, frozen, useless, chastised, when I looked up and realized I was beside the American Library. I had no idea such a thing existed, but it screamed "REFUGE!" to a very lost person.

To enter I had to show my passport, which I liked. There were Tanzanians there too, presumably students—presumably the real variety—with

some kind of pass, and a couple stray Americans. The collection was modest, three or four rooms lined with low bookshelves and half the volumes
facing forward. American history and political thought. The inescapable
Civil War and World War II sections. American artists, playwrights, poets,
and literature. I could hardly believe my hands, my dusty wanderer's hands,
when they picked up T.S. Eliot's *Selected Essays*. I knew Prufrock and
had struggled through "The Waste Land," but I had mostly been vaguely
repulsed by his low, steady heart rate, or perhaps just intimidated by his
vocabulary. At a hard wooden desk on a hard wooden chair and next to
a trembling air conditioner, I read "Tradition and the Individual Talent,"
alternately gripped and slipping back into my thoughts about what I was
doing here at all, and whether reading Eliot—Eliot in Africa!—meant I
had given up on Tanzania entirely and the dream of discovering myself in
the world, or was I just catching my breath?

The second book I pulled was by a poet, Mark Strand, whose name I
vaguely recognized. There was something about the tall, narrow cut of this
book published the year of my birth, the contrasting deep red above the royal
blue that called to me, and the title, *Reasons for Moving*, seemed to promise an answer to questions I hadn't yet figured out how to ask. The poems
are mostly short, written in narrow lines, in a simple, declarative style that
allows the macabre and the surrealistic to creep into his world almost unannounced. In these poems it is always night, and Strand or his double is passing through it on bus or by train, or perhaps locked in a lonely vigil, trapped
inside his house, afraid to go out. The cumulative effect is a bit like touching
an outlet: unpleasant but suspiciously alluring. Everyone he meets is either
damaged or threatening; the Strand character himself weaves between the
two, in one poem the tormenter, in the next the haunted.

It is often difficult for me to read a new poet. I need time and repetition to adjust to the idiosyncrasies of their voice, maybe even to tolerate
their artifice, but that day I passed straight into *Reasons for Moving*. Rather
than struggling to grasp what was being said, each word came as an affir-
mation of something I already knew but had never been able to articulate.
Each next line had the inevitability of a conversation with your closest

friend. And as I continued to read, even that gap closed. It was as though I could speak each word just before I saw it, as though I was simultaneously reading and writing the poems themselves.

Finally I reached "Keeping Things Whole," a poem deep in this narrow book, and suddenly the entire failed day, this disastrous trip, made sense; fifty-five words that rounded my existence. It begins, "In a field / I am the absence / of field," a simple claim that captured the necessity of my displacement.

What I understood in that moment was that, like Strand himself, I was a kind of rolling void, a little emptiness in the middle of things. And although there remained a part of me that wanted desperately to be embraced by the world, to be recognized and celebrated by it, I understood that each place I'd go would need to push me on a little further down the road for it to steady itself. Only by rejecting my presence could other things, other places keep themselves whole.

I could have felt damned by this realization, but instead I was filled by a strange invigoration, a liberating clarity, a release from purpose. I would never be the kind of connective tissue that holds a place together, that creates bridges from one world to another, who is remembered fondly in his absence, a good citizen, but I also caught an elusive glimpse of how this strange negativity, this permanent dislocation, could become a source of poetry if I was willing to follow it.

THE BOOK OF DISQUIET

Darley, an unaccomplished British writer and schoolteacher living in Alexandria, Egypt, in the 1930s, has just delivered a lecture at the city library to a largely disinterested audience on "the Poet of the City," C.P. Cavafy. He had intended to use the lecture's modest fee to buy a new coat for Melissa, who is so poor she must dance with strangers to keep herself fed, but wandering back to their apartment Darley impulsively, selfishly stops at a little import shop and spends the fee instead on an extravagant Pandora's Box of Italian olives, which he opens on the spot. As he tastes the oily salt and dreams of Tuscany, Darley is confronted by a woman he recognizes from the lecture audience, who without invitation seats herself across from him and rips into his naïve, lazy reading of Cavafy. She is, of course, Justine— beautiful, wounded, sophisticated, cosmopolitan. So begins the first book in Lawrence Durrell's *Alexandria Quartet*.

Darley can barely defend his half-formed theories from Justine's analysis. His cleverness was meant to be admired, not questioned. But despite his fumbling, inarticulate replies, Justine treats Darley as though he actually has something to say and insists he meet her husband, Nessim Hoesini, an esteemed figure in Alexandria's business community. The three become fast, inseparable friends, and through Nessim and Justine, Durrell is welcomed into another Alexandria—an exotic tangle of Egyptians, Greeks, and Englishmen; Muslims, Christians, and Jews; artists, diplomats, and mystics; galas, brothels, and slums. It is a recurring moment in literature and an elusive dream in life: a door opens and the hero is welcomed in, transformed by experience, awakened to knowledge.

But of course, we don't get to knowledge without suffering. Darley and Justine begin their inescapable, guilt-wracked affair, an obsessive, joyless betrayal, which may or may not be evident to Nessim, who may or may not be murderously jealous. Clear-eyed Melissa knows full well; in a hunger strike of sorts she starts to waste away.

By the opening of *Balthazar*, the Quartet's second book, it has all come apart. Darley has fled to a Greek island with Melissa's child after the affair was exposed and Nessim extracted some revenge that has undone their private Alexandria. Living in solitude and the haze of memory, Darley has written *Justine* and sent a copy to Balthazar, an elderly Alexandrian Greek who was a guide to Justine's Gnostic studies. While Darley describes his affair with Justine as an epic love story and the defining experience of his life, Balthazar—hesitantly, cruelly, honestly—replies that for Justine it was in fact little more than a diversion, and his explanation becomes *The Quartet's* second book. According to Balthazar, Justine had used the unthreatening Darley to mask another, more serious affair with Pursewarden, a relatively minor character in *Justine*. Pursewarden mirrors Darley in many ways—an Englishman in Egypt, an author and teacher. But Pursewarden is a genuinely accomplished and possibly brilliant novelist; he's unburdened by sentimentality and has a capacity for truth-telling that borders on the sadistic. Pursewarden's suicide was a minor event in *Justine*; in *Balthazar*, it becomes the brutal climax.

Although Balthazar's reply shatters his own understanding of his great love affair, Darley cannot deny that it is at least as plausible an account as his own.

Mountolive, the third book, offers yet another alternative reading of the same nexus of friends and events: while Justine had affairs with both Darley and Pursewarden, she always remained fundamentally bound to Nessim through their secret political endeavors to support Zionist militants, a side of Justine and Nessim that had been hidden to both Darley and Balthazar. If a second reading (*Balthazar*) suggests any of our assumptions could be false, a third (*Mountolive*), which implicitly presupposes a fourth, fifth, etc., suggests not just that we might have it wrong, but that there is no way to ever get to the Truth: there is always another truth beyond the one we've grasped, and each subsequent truth undermines what we thought we had known.

Only in the final book, *Clea*, does Time step forward: the War is over, and Darley returns to a battered Alexandria and surveys the devastation: Nessim in exile, Pursewarden and Melissa dead, Justine a gaunt, obscene figure. Darley, meanwhile, has survived and emerged, no longer the novice overwhelmed and deceived by events but a man able to understand the oddity of his own world, to move through it, to turn it into art.

I read and reread *The Alexandria Quartet* over three years in my early twenties while I was living in Prague and trying to establish myself as a writer. I had come straight out of college, drawn to the thrill of a new post-Soviet world while also believing that in such a place I might be able support myself while living a poet's life. I received a boost out the door from a college professor, a goateed fellow who balanced his limp with a silver-topped cane and frequently wore a black cape. As a babe, Andrew had been taken by his American communist parents to Czechoslovakia in 1950 to be raised on the right side of the Iron Curtain. That all went fine in its way until 1968 when their son, then a college student, was swept up in the revolutionary fervor of the times and became too visible in anti-government protests. The easiest solution for the state was to brand him a reactionary spy and kick him out of the country, and so he ended up back in the US where he eventually became an anthropologist with an affection for abstract thought specializing in the emergence of nation states in Central Europe. By the time I was graduating, however, revolution actually had come to most of the old Soviet Block, and suddenly my professor's old friends from the classrooms and the streets had become the department chairs and deans of the university. With his letter of introduction, I secured a position teaching English at Charles University's School of Journalism.

In my apartment on Skorepka, a one-block street nestled between Charles Bridge and the Old Town Square that was universally known to Czechs as the Street of Prostitutes, I set up a little shelf of books atop my dresser, about a dozen or so, many of which have remained part of my pantheon to this day. Borges' *Labyrinths*, Stephen Mitchell's ecstatic translation of Rilke, Cavafy's poems, Basho's *Narrow Road to the Deep North*, Yannis Ritsos' *Repetitions, Testimonies, Parentheses*, Louise Glück's *The Triumph of Achilles*, Jack Gilbert's *The Great Fires*, Linda Gregg's *Too Bright to See*, Schulz's *The Cinnamon Shops*, the juxtaposed translations of Li Po and Tu Fu, Fernando Pessoa's *The Book of Disquiet*. Those were all versions of the tight books I myself wanted to write; the only really fat, juicy, truly escapist volume was Durrell's *Alexandria Quartet*.

I was well aware of *The Quartet's* limitations: the canned romanticism, clichés of the exotic East, the myopic divide of women between whores and saints. I knew that if I was training myself to be the greatest poet of the 21st century, it made little sense to immerse myself in a novel that was a bit embarrassing by the late 20th. Yet I found all *The Quartet's* faults forgivable, just as most of my friends are narcissistic or cheap or neurotic and yet I never really want to be with anyone else; what matters most is not our worst qualities but our best. And of course, I found the transformation of Darley from a naïve pup to a man-of-the-world oddly convincing.

It was a shelf notably, troublingly devoid of Czechs. Rilke and Kafka had both lived here, of course, but they were German writers. I'd read, as everyone had back then, Milan Kundera, and I'd been charmed by Bohumil Hrabal's *I Served the King of England*, but I hadn't packed either, nor had I tracked down the other names I had begun to hear, Karel Capek, Miroslav Holub, Jachym Topol, Arnost Lustig. Had I read them, if I could talk about them knowingly in cafés and pubs, I imagined I'd have been welcomed with open arms by the Czechs, who'd recognize me as not-really-American and with whom I'd drink Moravian wines and argue politics and poetry. Some of them, presumably, would be women with endless Slavic names and cheekbones. I wanted that very badly. Instead, I was sleeping from time to time and with a mutual lack of conviction with another American. But I had also begun to understand that I needed something else as well, a kind of solitude or even fertile ignorance, so that in my deafness to the immediate world around me these other voices—Durrell, Borges, Basho, Calvino—could speak more clearly.

I lived on the top floor of my building, up four flights of wide, stone stairs that echoed with every step, no matter how carefully I climbed. As I passed, I could see a little flicker behind the brass peepholes on the doors, the hidden babushkas troubled by my presence. Although we rarely met or spoke, we lived together in curious ways, sharing, for example, a single phone line for the eight apartments, and choked plumbing that when I drained my tub would ultimately push my bath water, which I had heated pot by pot upon the stove, up through the sinks of the ground floor apartments with coffee grounds and cabbage rinds, quickly followed by a furious old woman banging on my door.

One afternoon I came home and it was raining in my apartment, as though the ceiling had become a single, soaked cloud coming apart in huge torrents, filling the rugs, pooling on the floor and sinking down into the unit below. Workers had come that day to replace the roof tiles, but when they'd broken for lunch, the job half done, a storm blew in and rather than hurry back to create some kind of cover, they—loyal to the finest Czech values—remained at the pub, shaking their heads at the exhausting absurdity of it all. When it finally passed and I'd mopped the water from the floor and propped the mattress and pillows to dry, when after days the moisture finally evaporated from the room, the plaster ceiling began to crack like a dried-up river bed, and, as though it were a dead fish, flies buzzed around the burnt-out dangling bulb.

Other than my books, my most intimate companion was not the beautiful Slovak professor with whom I shared an office but Vaclav Fisher, the World War II vet whose apartment I rented and who would leave his cottage outside of Pilsen and come, unannounced, uninvited, to stay with me for a couple nights every few weeks. Ownership meant something different there, and even though I was renting his apartment, he felt perfectly welcome to stay in it from time to time. He was even lonelier than me, and I remember my sinking feeling when I'd return home, put the key in the lock, and its mere quarter turn would tell me he was there, waiting to talk. Each time he came prepared with a bottle of cheap vodka or brown rum and a few lukewarm beers that he insisted I share with him while we slowly drank ourselves into a stupor. All his friends were dead.

Fisher spoke to me in German, a language I could sometimes understand but rarely speak, which suited us both. He told me about the four heart attacks and the two strokes (or possibly it was the other way around) that hadn't been able to kill him. He took some pride in that. He showed me his library of pills, never explaining what they were for but going into great detail about what each one cost. We shared an antagonism toward doctors.

Eventually the afternoon would wear on and the bottles would empty and he'd realize that I'd been nodding along to whatever he'd been saying without really tracking it. That would make him mad, or at least dramatic. He'd feign hurt. No one, not even me, understood him. He was alone! If he could have stood up, he'd have stormed out. I'd wake up at that point and piece together a couple sentences, but he'd just shake his head. He'd wave his huge hand to swat me away.

But he couldn't resist an audience, even an inattentive one, and soon enough he'd try to lure me back into whatever story he was telling. Once, he wanted me to know, he was just like me, by which he meant, I believe, young, healthy, maybe something more. That was in Germany, where he spent the war in a work camp. He showed me his teeth, but I'm not sure why. He told me about the many women he'd had. On his fingers he'd count: French. Dutch. Russian. Hungarian. Polish. He'd tell me about the disappointment of his children. He suspected there were as many as two hundred of them, spread across Europe, but I only ever met the exhausted Dasha, who would occasionally come to clean up after him.

Sometimes when he'd arrive I'd have a friend visiting, and if it happened to be a woman he'd brighten up immediately, doing his best to hide the years. He had a kind of playful sparkle that must have made him quite charming at some point. After telling a few jokes neither of us quite got, he would awkwardly pantomime that if we wanted to be alone, he would stay in the kitchen.

One morning I thought he was having the heart attack that would finally kill him off. At the sound of his gasping, I rushed to his side. He was leaning over the table with one arm holding himself upright, pounding himself in the chest with the other, trying to cough or reboot his heart.

Suddenly, I could speak German: "Should I call your daughter? The hospital?" Already my mind was racing to how I might possibly do that.

"No," he gasped, "the bottle." While his eyes wobbled like two soft-boiled eggs, I uncorked the rum and wrapped his paws around it. Intuitively, he lifted the bottle to his lips and he gulped his way half through it, soaking his chin and lap. Then he burped, a deep, medieval burp, a Rabelaisian belch of life. Steadying himself, he smiled at his own indestructibility. My Fisher was no Justine.

But he was sweet, in his strange ways. I picture him seated at the kitchen table, the room barely lit but for the blue light of the four burners on the stove, which he used for heat, giving everything a drowsy, gassy haze. He liked me not just because I would listen but also because people sent me letters from foreign countries. I'd clip the stamps for him. He insisted they were for his grandson, but the only time he'd put on his glasses was to inspect my offering, and if I'd been a little careless and had nicked the ridged trim, he made sure to point that out so I'd be more careful next time.

It was a perfect place to write and at last the stories, poems and letters came pouring out of me.

On days I taught, I'd often begin at the Café Slavika, a grand Art Nouveau coffeehouse across from the opera on the Vltava River, a few blocks down from the School of Journalism. When I was reading *The Alexandria Quartet*, there were days when I could swirl the two cities in my mind, Alexandria's cool Mediterranean-sea mist stirred into Prague's brown coal haze like cream into coffee; clock towers into minarets. I was always myself, but I was also Darley, so full of promise, so short of achievements. And in all the women who circled around me were alternating currents of Justine, Melissa, Clea. Those days everything became layered with meaning, with possibilities.

For a while, though, I'd been reading instead Fernando Pessoa's *The Book of Disquiet*. If Durrell projected something I was hoping to reach—cosmopolitan intrigue, initiation, sex—Pessoa was much closer to my daily existence in Prague. After a ten-year childhood sojourn in South Africa that he never mentioned in any of the many things he wrote, Pessoa spun out his life in his native Lisbon, where he worked as a freelance clerk translating commercial documents for a dozen import/export businesses.

He lived in a rented room and took his meals in modest restaurants that catered to bachelors. Despite being obsessively observant, he had a hard time making eye contact, especially with women, though he did manage to become engaged to the lovely Ophelia Queiroz. In one of his more seductive letters, he wrote, "If I marry, it will only be to you. It remains to be seen whether marriage and a home (or whatever else you want to call it) are things that are sufficient for my life and the way I think. I doubt it." He wore suits, a broad-rimmed hat, and a narrow, well-trimmed mustache. He was troubled by homosexuals.

Mostly he read poetry and philosophy. With his small, soon-spent inheritance, he set up an experimental publishing house, Empreza Ibis, which failed. A few years later he launched *Orpheu*, a small literary journal that extinguished itself after producing just two issues but which is credited nonetheless with introducing modernist literature to Portugal.

What friends he had were mostly writers and future suicides, a fate he surprisingly escaped as he was prone to thoughts like, "I've always considered living a metaphysical mistake on the part of matter." Or: "Yes, tedium is boredom with the world, the malaise of living, the weariness of having lived; in truth, tedium is the feeling in one's flesh of the endless emptiness of things. But, more than that, tedium is a boredom with other worlds, whether they exist or not; the malaise of living, even if one were someone else, with a different life, in another world; a weariness not just with yesterday or today, but with tomorrow too, with all eternity (if it exists) and with nothingness (if that is what eternity is)..."

What's most remarkable about Pessoa is that on March 8, 1914, four months before the launch of World War I, when he was thirty-two and a general disappointment, he stood beside a high chest of drawers—his preferred writing position—and churned out some thirty poems, one after another. They were unlike anything he'd ever written before: simple, clear poems, calmly accepting the world around us rather than seeking to analyze or crawl beneath the surface.

It was immediately obvious to him that these poems were not written by "Fernando Pessoa." Just to be certain, he wrote six more poems that were in fact by Fernando Pessoa, and they sounded entirely different. What's even more surprising is that he knew who had written them—Alberto Caeiro, who was born in 1889, a year after Pessoa, and who had lived almost all his life in the country, without a profession or any formal education. Through Pessoa, Caeiro would go on to write scores of poems, including those collected in *The Keeper of Sheep*, and even develop a cult following and imitators. And that was just the start.

In the crowded house of Pessoa's mind, there had always been other characters, but once Caeiro emerged he was soon joined by Ricardio Reis, Alexander Search, the Chevalier de Pas, Charles Robert Anon, and other fully formed poets and philosophers—at least seventy-two have left some trace. One of the most prolific and accomplished was Alvaro de Campos, a Whitmanesque seer able to fully embrace his own feelings and, through his expansive soul, embrace the staggering totality of existence. He was born a year after Caeiro in 1890, and spent much of his life in Glasgow, though he also lived in Lisbon and traveled to the Orient as a naval engineer.

Pessoa's many "heteronyms," as he called them to distinguish them from more simplistic pseudonyms, wrote poetry and essays of course, but they also lived full, independent lives, or at least accumulated complex biographies—some with rigorous Jesuit educations, others self-taught and sloppy in their grammar. They were shepherds, doctors, monarchists, exiles, false pagans, sad epicures. Sometimes they reviewed each other's works, sparking both mutual adoration and bitter feuds. For someone who lived alone, with few intimates, they became a kind of society of exiles; not friends per se, but anchors in reality, confidants, rivals.

The heteronym most similar to Pessoa himself was Bernardo Soares, a remote bachelor, a classic early 20th-century flaneur who wandered the streets of Lisbon, observing and relentlessly over-interpreting everything that passed before him, surrounded by lives he'd never participate in or only momentarily cross, and whose notebooks comprise *The Book of Disquiet*.

Just as I longed to live within the rich, incestuous community of Durrell's Alexandria, I felt a parallel envy of the inside of Pessoa's head and its multitudes—how complete, I imagined, it must feel to have all those alternatives rising up through you, insisting to be heard. But even more than that, as a young poet who felt myself continually tumbling through ideas and voices rather than genuinely inhabiting any of them, it was a wonderful temptation to believe that what kept me from greatness was my inability to untangle possibilities, that the reason everything I wrote felt, just a few days later, muddled and insincere, was because there were too many artists inside me, stumbling over one another. If I could only sort them out, set each one beside the other, as Pessoa had done, then perhaps all these words inside me would also unravel into elegant, heartbreaking lines. And then some night I'd come home to my kitchen table and write thirty poems, a complete break from everything I'd ever written before, and they'd endure.

Wandering the streets, the cafés, the low-end restaurants of Lisbon, Soares would observe memorable characters like the wry, pockmarked Faustino Antunes, a renowned seducer of widowed women, or Abilio Quaresma, a barber with a prized touch for masking bald spots and receding hairlines, but the more constant theme of *The Book of Disquiet* is the divide between Soares' wandering thoughts, which are intricate, rich, and fertile, and the blank dullness of the actual world to which he's been consigned. With its strict tensions between the internal and external, it is a book best read in public, surrounded by strangers. I liked to read it sitting beside a well-cleaned window at the Café Slavika over a bitter espresso. When I'd finish a passage—most of which are only a few paragraphs long though dense and unresolved—I'd lean back and watch others through the window passing on the street with a satisfying anonymity. Office workers, students, repairmen, Gypsies, old women, nurses. Not every day but often enough I'd eventually glimpse some recognizable one within the crowd, a woman I had stood behind in a checkout line or a man I'd noticed giving up his seat on a tram. I liked to imagine then how our looping, nonlinear paths, like an impossibly knotted spool of thread meant to guide us through the labyrinth, trailed out behind us from this moment to our first crossing. Some days I felt like I was waiting for an old, lost friend, a former lover, to step out of the street's swollen mass and back into my life. But that never happened.

As I sipped my coffee and abandoned the outside world, I might turn my discreet gaze back on my fellow patrons of the café, those of us who'd stepped out of the world and into this stillness, if only for a little while. One of the great luxuries of not speaking Czech very well was that even though the people around me were undoubtedly exchanging mundane realities, I could always imagine that their conversations were shameful or erotic, or best—shamefully erotic. In all likelihood, that couple was discussing what they'd have for dinner that night, and who would pick what up on the way home, but the possibility remained that she was, at last, confessing to him about the boy she had once loved who'd died in a snow drift, or even better, how she liked to be touched. And if each of these unwitting Czechs could be transformed into someone else, why couldn't I as well? What would it take for me to become Bernardo Soares, that haunter of cafés and half-darkened streets, the true author of Pessoa's *Book of Disquiet*? Then, just as Soares might pass almost unnoticed through his world, remembered at best as a simple bookkeeper who rarely made a clerical mistake while secretly recording the most extraordinary thoughts, maybe I could similarly be dismissed as the most average of English teachers and as a haunter of side streets and cafés while filling my private journal with words and observations that would still be treasured a hundred years into the future.

Turning back to *The Book of Disquiet*, I read that "someone afflicted by tedium feels himself the prisoner of a futile freedom, in a cell of infinite size."

The last dregs of my coffee were cold, and surely other colleagues and students had begun to make their appearance at the university. I had come to dread teaching, facing the disappointment of this incredible generation whose lives would be so very different from their parents', who were so curious, so hungry to experience the western world—of which I was always an underwhelming simulacrum. People who were so much more interesting in all likelihood than the strangers around me, but who had the frustrating quality of being real, and it was their insistent reality, coupled with the turning of the clock, that pushed Pessoa out of my head, breaking the spell. With that, I closed up my notebook. I tapped the little spoon against my espresso saucer as though it were a chime closing this loop. I put on my overcoat, buttoning it to the very top; I smoothed my non-existent mustache. Then I stepped out into the street.

* * *

If my days were filled with fantasies inspired by Durrell and Pessoa of an infinite city swirling around the little star of my self, fantasies of my plastic mind giving voice to a pantheon of poets, the nights were harder, the hours longer and less obedient to my whims. Although it's inviting to think of the darkness as a carnival where we can become something else under the cover of its shadows, it was in the lonely hours of night when I felt most inescapably, most disappointingly myself. Sometimes I'd wander Prague's circling alleys until I'd walked the sun down, and other times I'd join with friends and drink myself into the black hours, but there were many more evenings I spent alone in that crumbling apartment, looking down from my window at the exchanges being negotiated below. Amid the peeling linoleum kitchen, I'd scrambled together some half-hearted dinner for one. There was no radio, no television, no telephone or internet, but I could read.

The poet of my nights was Rainer Maria Rilke, a native of Prague, born to a German-speaking family of Austrian descent, but of his own making a nationless person, unbound even to the wife and child he would continually leave behind. He spent most of his life on the cusp of poverty, living when he could as a guest of the fading aristocracy of the early 20th century, whether that meant in Russia, Germany, Spain, Italy, or France. Rilke's ruthless detachment from identities (and from responsibilities in general) freed him to experience the world around him with a perverse intimacy. His penetrating gaze would impregnate whatever became the focus of his attention—a panther, the dead, a limbless statue, that one twinkling star—with Meaning, and the simplest of encounters would leave him exhausted and sick. Many consider him the greatest poet of the last century.

He had an overwhelming impulse to worship, and a great capacity for it. This extended to the objects that inhabited his world as well as to the great men that defined it. As a young man, he made a pilgrimage to visit Leo

Tolstoy at his estate. It must have been a great disappointment when the old man, a champion of the 1,000-page novel, belittled Rilke's interest in the mere "lyric." He had greater success in Paris with the sculptor Rodin who took him on as a secretary, a job that left Rilke many hours for contemplation and which inspired some of his greatest early work. Before long, it was Rilke himself who was becoming the sought-after and admired one, both by a string of older, often widowed gentlewomen with grandiose names like Alice Fahndrich von Nordeck zur Rabenau or the Countess Margot Sizzo-Noris Crouy, as well as by aspiring poets. His responses to one such man, Franz Xaver Kappus, collected as Rilke's *Letters to a Young Poet*, have developed a cult-like following over the decades, a staple of both writing retreats and self-actualization seminars. Rilke repeatedly warns young Kappus that no one can advise him, that he must go deep into himself if he's to discover any truth, but that caveat is quickly followed, letter after letter, by sage thoughts about the artist's life, the necessity of solitude and pain, about love. Each time I notice it, I'm caught off guard by the realization that Rilke himself was only in his late twenties when these gospels began, which I assume means he was writing them as much to his wavering self as to any named other.

Sitting at my kitchen table below a light fixture dimmed by dust, I re-read Rilke's *New Poems* and become another awed witness to the intensity of his experience. I knew, from the unexpected line breaks and jarring punctuation, the juxtaposed images, how each of his nerve-ends tingled with longing. It was beautiful. It was masterful. And yet...there always remained some barrier between us, some extravagance of thought that wanted me to remain its witness rather than coconspirator. With Durrell or Pessoa, I often reached some moment of transference, in which reading them allowed me, if only for some moments, to inhabit their beings. But Rilke was always a glittering someone else, always out of reach.

All readers at times feel as though they've been written to directly, even across the years and by others who never knew their name but who somehow sensed their inevitability. Some nights, I felt that way with Rilke. He's had that power over many. And what he said stung. That I had been consigned to the surface of things, and that shallowness was my purgatory.

That I'd never feel real joy, or even suffering for that matter, that I couldn't. He'd dare me: when would I follow him and become a raw nerve, an emptiness waiting to be filled, a saint without a god to serve? He went deeper and deeper into himself, howling in the void.

If I read too much of him one night, he might follow me the next day, with his heavy eyelids, his sickly pallor, slowly shaking his head as I haunted cafés and streets, as I flickered through identities, donning masks so I could have any expression at all. He made my proud doppelgangering look cheap; not artful, not daring, but cowardly. And so while I wrote simple, shallow things, clever poems that captured the little absurdity of little moments, he, from the depths of his singular mind, produced line after line like this: "Who, if I cried out, would hear me among the angels' / hierarchies? and even if one of them pressed me / suddenly against his heart: I would be consumed / in that overwhelming existence." Oh, I heard him.

Undoubtedly in an attempt to match his lyricism, to claim some sliver of it myself, sometimes in the loneliness of my long evenings, on those nights when I'd come home from whatever it was that had failed to hold me there, I'd survey my apartment, trying to lure each thing into some heightened existence, into Meaning. Rusty faucets, the coal smoke-stained wall above the heater, the crumb rolling off my table into some unknown void: all ripe with possibilities, all unwritten poems. Rilke would nudge me toward them. And watch.

But I could never quite fully wrap that Rilkean cloak around my shoulders, perhaps because even in the dark loneliness of my nights, especially in the dark loneliness of my nights, when I was finally circling his depths, I'd picture him reading his poem about a mirror quivering orgasmically with his memory to a bejeweled noblewoman on her desperate quest for purpose, and rather than gasp, I'd feel myself snicker. Good god, I thought, just fuck her already. Although it was clear there were all kinds of voids within me, I knew that at least a few of them echoed with a liberating lack of seriousness, with the tin drum beat of absurdity, with laughter—a particular sound that poor Rilke could never make. And his spell, at least for the evening, would be broken.

BETWEEN THE WOODS AND THE WATER

My biggest fear when I was six years old and told that we would move to Iowa was that I would need to learn a new language. Iowan? I had just learned English and already I was being asked to do the impossible. My mom and I rode out together in the family station wagon a few days behind my sister and dad who'd driven the U-Haul. Despite my fears, my mom was in a cheery mood, singing Willie Nelson and Waylon Jennings tunes the entire way, transporting herself into another world. When we arrived on Templin Road my sister Jenny was clearly shell-shocked, which I assumed meant she had accepted the truth at last about how far we had gone, about the terrible mistake our parents had made.

She told me: while our dad had unloaded the truck, Jenny had milled about. The neighborhood kids had all kept a safe distance for a while, watching her through the hedges, across the yards, whispering, pointing. When they finally sent forward an emissary, the little redhead informed Jenny they were keeping an eye on her because our new house had previously belonged to the family of another young girl about my sister's age, Phoebe, who had crucified her pet monkey in her backyard. Her family had been obliged to leave town, and we were destined to be "the kids who lived in Phoebe's house."

By the time school began a couple hot months later, Jenny and I had learned the mile-long walk across the band field, down River Street and through Manville Heights to Lincoln Elementary, and in the mornings we, having pledged not to sacrifice anyone's dog or cat, were allowed to join the gaggle of neighborhood kids from—girls to one side of the street, boys to the other, slightly older kids half a block ahead.

It was there at the corner of River and Magowan Avenue that young, proud Helena Mackenzie, with her August blond hair and golden skin, with her beautiful, swan neck, entered my world. She was wearing a blue summer dress and a tinfoil crown bedazzled with beads and buttons. Having arrived with her family from London, she had let her newfound, first-grade subjects know their place by insisting she was going to become the Queen of England, and thus she had to dress the part. I felt a disconcerting, unnamable pang in my chest, which may have been healed or more likely ripped apart had she only turned her regal head my way.

Young romantics have a hard time retaining focus, and it's true that after a few confused days the unknown emotions I felt in her presence simmered out and before long Helena was just another snot-nosed playground girl with skinned knees and a tiara, but they never quite disappeared, resurfacing in odd ways, such that, for example, the first two girls I ultimately dated were named Elena and Ellen, which seemed like asking for trouble, especially for a tongue-tied dyslexic with a history of speech impediments. Through years of tutoring, I'd become an able reader, but I still couldn't spell at all, not to please a teacher or impress a girl. I remember once romantically notching "CH + AS" into a junior high desk, and then my deep shame as I realized Elena Zlatnik was an EZ, not an AS.

In our small town surely we crossed in various classes, track meets, and awkward school dances, but it wasn't until I was seventeen that I really saw Helena again, when she had become everything the beautiful little girl on the corner had promised. No longer a future queen, she was a full princess of the prairie, olive toned, skinny, and tough from riding horses across her family's fields outside of town, or jetting through the streets on a rickety moped with a camera strapped across her shoulder on assignment for the school paper, her asymmetrical 1980s hair aflutter, and all those first feelings came back, as confused and inarticulate as when I was six.

Bumbling toward her with the grace of an agitated colt, I accidentally half-dated one of her closest friends. The intense rage I saw in her eye when she dramatically kicked me out of a party at her house after I showed up with another girl filled me with hope. Our orbits were intertwining; gravity pulled. One troublesome spring night, Helena, her boyfriend, and I drove to the drive-in theater outside town and to save a few bucks or simply to test our deviance, we tucked Mark away in the trunk of my car at the entry, then she and I drove around the parking lot for a while with him locked up. When we flirted, she would give me her half-smile, which I came to accept as part of her pride—that even when something amused her, she wouldn't give herself over to it entirely.

When we kissed for the first time, it had none of the romanticism that epochal moment deserved. In a field of wild flowers? On a Scottish moor, rekindling some past illicit Hamilton / Mackenzie coupling? No, in Joe Kimura's foul, parent-forsaken basement, at the end of another frustrated teen-age party when I'd been unable, despite the weed and booze, to cross the minefield of desire and fear that separated us, when she took my hand and pulled me down onto a couch. After a slow, frightened kiss she leaned back, just slightly, so she could look at me more closely, into my eyes, trying to find something—but I've never known just what, or if it was there.

In the weeks that followed—the last of high school—I felt all the things I'd read so much about but had never genuinely known: how the slightest, even falsely imagined shift in her emotions could ripple through me joyfully or with pain; the electric touch of her fingers. But to my dismay my mom had planned a trip for the two of us—a graduation present—to Italy where she had spent a magical summer as a teen and which she now wanted to share with me. For once in my life the only place I wanted to be was in Iowa. On the night before my mom tore me away, I, quivering with fear, with Helena already in her car, the engine already rumbling, told her that I loved her.

She considered my words for a moment and then whispered, "So do I," quite convincingly, before adding, "myself, that is." And then that cruel girl sped away.

For the next three weeks as I did my best to be thoroughly unimpressed by Florence, Rome, and Venice, my mom and I fought. What were their beauties compared to Helena's? Dirty old buildings versus hot young flesh? This trip was meant to bind my mom and I together, but I was a continent away. I wrote unanswerable letters. I spent my money on a necklace I doubted she'd wear. I pointed out all the Germans. My mom marched ahead furiously and appreciated art. Soon we were eating meals in silence. Her moods had always frightened me, and she had plenty of proof that if she acted wounded enough she'd eventually cow me into submission and an apology, but this time it didn't work. Nothing she could do was a match for the possibility of Helena's indifference. Our delicate balance of power was tilting. The flight home, trapped side by side, must have rounded the planet twice.

As fast as I could, I drove out to Helena's, where it took her a bug's lifetime to answer the door. I kept wiping my palms on my shorts. When she finally answered, we looked at each other for a moment, fixed on two sides of the frame, letting the clichés wash over us—myself in the sun, Helena in shadows.

We spent the rest of the summer as only young lovers can—creating secret codes meant to bind us forever, feeling things that no human had ever felt, fucking athletically, artlessly in every hidden nook and cranny the city would offer up, making unkeepable promises. One afternoon we both had our astrological signs read and were triply confused when Helena was told that she would be the writer, that I should move to Brazil, and we wouldn't spend our lives together. Through it all, the sun was sinking, and we both knew that at the end of August she would move to California for college and I was bound for the East Coast. We assured each other that our love was different and would last.

* * *

Six years later, I made a trip home from Prague for my mom's second wedding in Philadelphia and then on to Iowa City to visit my dad over New

Year's. Helena was back in town too, from San Francisco where she'd been living after college, to visit her mom.

We hadn't spoken for a while, though since I'd been abroad, we wrote letters to each other now and then, me trying to explain about the life I was putting together, the things I was writing; she as she thought about law school or perhaps psychology. We discreetly avoided mentioning the other people in our lives except in vague, belittling terms. Our romance had exploded miserably early in the first year of college, when I got a dispiriting glimpse of how fickle even my most intense emotions can be, as all the love and lust I'd felt for Helena kept surging up through me but attaching itself instead to those closer by. After saying some horrible things, we didn't talk for a long time, but slowly that too faded, and we'd reconciled in a conditional way, so that throughout college summers and holidays, when we'd both be home from our respective coasts, we'd often end up sleeping together. That New Year's, however, I was very much alone and Helena was trying to get out of a relationship that was proving to be more resilient than rewarding.

That fall I'd read two favorites of my mom's, Patrick Leigh Fermor's *A Time of Gifts* and *Between the Woods and the Water*, co-joining travelogues that begin in 1933 when eighteen-year-old Patrick, after failing out of several schools, including one for difficult children, and after being recognized by a teacher for his "dangerous mixture of sophistication and recklessness," a description that filled me with aching envy, began to walk—still trying to find the action that matched his restless ambitions—across Europe, from the Hook of Holland through Germany, Czechoslovakia, Hungary, the Balkans, Romania, and ultimately to Constantinople, as he insisted on calling it. He had an allowance of a pound a week, which was only enough if he were to survive on the cheap. He slept in monasteries, barns and shepherds' huts, but by the time he entered Central Europe, he'd also charmed his way into a network of old aristocracy—the same network Rilke had discovered—that was clearly amused by this adventurous young Brit, and under their care, he left each country estate or city chateau with a letter of introduction to the next set of cousins or countrymen a little further down the way until he reached Constantinople in 1935. The walk had stirred rather than quenched his appetite for exploration, and instead of heading home he continued from Turkey into Greece, where he would mostly remain through the Second World War, helping to lead the resistance in Crete and participating in the daring, although irresponsible and not entirely helpful, capture of the German General Heinrich Kreipe.

In a wonderful twist of literary fate, Fermor had kept a meticulous journal of his long walk but then accidently left one volume of his diary behind in a Romanian castle, which before long was separated by an Iron Curtain. When it was returned to him decades later, the memories came cascading back and he finally wrote these incredible travelogues—more than forty years after the journey itself, and long after the world he had explored had effectively ceased to exist.

Still dizzy and reckless from sex, I made a proposition to Helena that New Year's Eve. Why didn't she meet me in Prague the next summer and together we'd walk from Gdansk at the southern tip of the Baltics through Lithuania, Latvia, and Estonia to Tallinn, where, by August, the sun would barely set?

Ready to change her life, and perhaps to call me out as all talk, she said why not?

This was, of course, a spur-of-the-moment offer, and while I was perfectly genuine in wanting to be with Helena, I hadn't actually looked at a map and had only the vaguest idea of how long a trip we were talking about, or what the northern Baltics—which in my dyslexic mind I still confuse with the southern Balkans—are like. It turns out it is about 600 miles from Gdansk to Tallinn, somewhat longer if we were to adhere to the coastline. If we were to aim for about ten miles a day and allow for the occasional bus or train to make a little leap forward, we could certainly make it in six to eight weeks, even with a bit of lingering in Vilnius or Riga. And on top of everything else, a few American dollars still went a long way in the former USSR, and what the two of us could save from our odd jobs before summer would probably sustain us.

Throughout the spring, I wrote Helena often, sprinkling my letters with lines of awful love poetry and memories of the sex I'm pretty sure I'd had with her. Her replies were more level-headed, but the letter I expected, the one where she announced that she'd come to her senses, met someone better, never arrived. Instead, she did. As a six-year-old, I'd fallen for Helena from across the street. Now, with a hot cocktail of hormones jostling my senses, I greeted her at the airport, breathing in her singular scent as I hugged her muscular, Californian self to me. I thought: this is exactly the trouble I want.

* * *

She was a reader too. The summer when Helena and I had first dated, we would buy two copies of a single title from one of Iowa City's many used bookstores, *The Book of Laughter and Forgetting*, *The World According to Garp*, *London Fields*. When we were peeled apart by other realities, we'd read our shared books and when we came back together, we'd catch up on what had happened in our parallel worlds. That was too sweet for this still suspicious reunion, but I had brought along Italo Calvino's *Invisible Cities* as well as Marco Polo's *Travels*, and in the leisure of our evenings or over a midmorning coffee, I'd read to her snippets of Calvino.

Invisible Cities is structured as a series of brief exchanges between Kublai Khan, emperor of a vast and unknowable realm, and one of the many ambassadors the Khan sends out to report back from his frontiers, Marco Polo. At first, being a foreigner, Marco can't speak the Khan's language and so he must describe the cities through a series of gestures, props, and pantomimes, which the Khan deciphers but always with a degree of uncertainty—perhaps what was intended was something else entirely. Who can really say whether the chessboard queen Polo maneuvers is meant to represent a lady looking down from her balcony, a fountain, a church with a pointed dome, or a quince tree?

It is particularly difficult because the cities Polo describes are so incredible, so unlike, at least on the surface, any city the Khan has ever visited. Opulent cities (as only a cunning merchant could describe them) filled with nutmeg, ginger, fishing poles, saffron, golden muslin. But mostly just strange cities, each defined by its particular mutation from the norm: a city where not just goods but also memories are traded. A city that is constantly being rebuilt from its own scraps, so that curtains and funeral urns and bar stools are endlessly repurposed into something else. A city that rises up into the sky on stilts, and another, mirrored city burrowing into the earth below. A city you can return to after many years and find precisely the same conversations occurring, although the people having them have changed entirely.

Over time, as the two come to understand each other better, the Khan begins to suspect that each of these cities is only a fantasy of Polo's, and even worse, that the great explorer never actually travels anywhere at all but simply conjures grand illusions from his imagination to deceive the Emperor. Or that every city Polo describes is simply a different reflection of his beloved and lost Venice. But every time the Khan thinks he has figured out Polo's game and could perhaps master it himself, the elusive Polo changes the rules or slips out of logic's grasp, continuing his travels, real or imagined, through the unknown cities of the realm.

It was a tempting game, and to keep ourselves amused—and perhaps because Helena shared my inability to ever fully be wherever I was—we wondered what Calvino's Polo would have told his Khan about the places we visited. What did it mean that Cracow, an ancient seat of learning, birthplace of the Pope, now had a pizza parlor on every corner and an Italian shoe store nestled in each block? Or that Gdansk, where the Solidarity movement that ruptured the Soviet grip was launched, had gone back to the simple work of loading and unloading ships? And what to say about Vilnius, a town Napoleon crowned the Jerusalem of the North, with its ninety-two synagogues and not a Jew to be found? The way, if we aren't very vigilant, time allows the trivial and the traumatic to attain equal weight. These remote Baltics were among the last outposts in Europe to be Christianized, only falling to Jesus in 1200 after a northern crusade, and less than a hundred years later the Mongols were on their border.

One of the wonderful and often overlooked oddities of *The Travels of Marco Polo* is that they were not written by Marco Polo, who was probably hardly literate despite speaking a dozen languages native to the markets of the world, but rather by a medieval court poet, Rustichello of Pisa, and it's likely they never would have been written at all if fate hadn't landed Polo and Rustichello in a shared Genoese prison cell. After twenty-six years in the East, Polo traveled 8,000 miles back from the heart of the Mongol Empire and was nearly in sight of his beloved Venice when his ship was seized by the Genoese, who were fighting the Venetians for trade routes. He was a highly suspicious character and the simplest place to store him was in jail. What landed Rustichello, a poet, behind bars is less clear; perhaps his verses had managed to offend the Prince or to seduce the wrong woman? Whatever the reason, it was one of history's fertile mashups—an Ambassador of the Great Khan locked away with a hack writer of courtly romances. How long until Rustichello realized he'd been chained to his long-awaited muse? How long until Polo, stripped at the border of all his goods, realized he had something extraordinary still to trade?

Though it was high summer, it rained everywhere we went along that troubled coast: cold, penetrating rain. To warm ourselves, or pass the time, as we walked a trail in northern Poland, I described to Helena how prison must have been sheer torture for Rustichello, with the narrow view down from the tower. It was spring, and life below sounded so gay. He could hear the women laughing to be teased and imagined their whispered replies. But where was the vigil? Where was the mourning that these good citizens had been denied his company? His friends? His past and future lovers? The narrow window was a cruel reminder how effortlessly life below had gone on in his absence.

Then she picked up the story, turning it over. Unlike Rustichello, Polo, she imagined, could stare for hours down at the market below. Although his life had been spent between one city and the next, many of the journeys unfolded in cells of their own—a ship's cabin, a camel's back. While he may have been locked in a Genoese jail, he had a voyager's confidence that he was continuing to travel through days, which in the end are not so different from cities or the long stretches of land that divide them. To pass the time, he tried to count the coins as they passed from hand to hand below, teaching himself the value here of linen and carp. Nothing pleased him more than to observe a con. And when he was most pleased, he couldn't keep himself from talking.

As Polo talked, he opened his hands on his lap, brushing his pants as though spreading a cloth upon which to display his wares. Polo claimed to have spent twenty-six years in the East. In the service of the Great Khan, Polo has traveled to Kashgar, to Beijing and Chengdu; he has survived shipwrecks, piracy, brigands, and beasts. His stories were unlike anything Rustichello had ever heard, but was any of it real? Rustichello had no way to know, and Polo, the sly trader, gave no clue. Perhaps these were the same stories everyone told in Jerusalem or Black Sea harbor bars. Rustichello was intrigued, but careful not to reveal his interest. This cell, he suspected, was a market too, and one he shared with a man who claims to have cheated Mongols of their ponies.

* * *

Poland was not so different from the realities I'd become accustomed to in Prague, but when we crossed into Kaliningrad, a small wedge of Russia tucked under Lithuania on the Baltic coast, our first step into the former Soviet Union, we were somewhere else. I'd grown used to some of the simpler expressions of a non-capitalist society, the absence, for example, of multiple brands or any choice between basic commodities. Soap was soap, soda was soda. Similarly, the notion that purchasing more, a larger bottle, a bigger burger, should entitle one to a discounted price—a defining belief of capitalist consumption—was anathema, as were the periodic sales that cleared the shelves and ushered in a new cycle of products. Or that there is no reason for a pregnancy test to come in a fancy, stylishly-designed and reassuring plastic tube when the only piece you really need is the fortune cookie-like slip of paper you could pinch between your fingers and pee upon.

But in Kaliningrad, the lack of pandering to consumers went a step further. Although we would have struggled enough with Cyrillic, there was a near complete absence of signage in any language in either the train station or on the streets themselves, and each building had the same expressionless façade. For all we could understand, behind any one of those doors we could find a butcher's, a men's chess club, a KGB listening station, or a deserted swimming pool swarming with lizards.

When I was still young enough to wear a Speedo on the beach, my family spent a winter vacation in the Yucatan splashing around the blue waters and exploring ruins. One night we were eating at an innocuous tourist restaurant when my dad turned an astonishing shade of white. With one palm he steadied himself against the table; with the other he held his chest. (The same pose, I realize now, I saw in Fisher ten years later.) Everyone, waiters included, went silent and watched. As though he were channeling a 1940s movie, he slurred, "I think someone slipped me a Mickey." And then he slumped over and fell. My mom insists that her first thought, even before he could hit the floor, was, "How am I going to get the body home?" She loved telling that story.

He was revived, of course, and when my dad left her a few years later, my mom was alone in a big house. My sister was in the Peace Corps and I was finishing college with no intention of ever going home. A less dramatic type would have gotten a dog or moved into a condo, but my mom was never one for half-gestures, so she adopted a young Russian couple, Anna and Tolya, who'd emigrated to the States on her student visa and were now dangling in a precarious legal limbo. Tolya was six and a half feet tall, or about twice my mother's size, and a former Soviet speed skater turned masseur. He did odd jobs around the house and yard while learning English the old-fashioned way, by watching daytime TV. Meanwhile Anna, who was six feet herself and fluent in multiple languages, snuck first into the Linguistics Department at the University of Iowa and then into the law school. She and my mom liked to cook together and walk. With my sister and I gone, they cared for her and she for them. When Anna learned that Helena and I would tour the Baltics, she insisted we visit her parents in Kaliningrad. Though it wasn't as grandiose as my grandfather receiving summons to the Tolstoy residence in Moscow, time was playing its little game with us, repeating patterns in a slightly degenerated form.

So there we were, outside the train station, frozen in place. The Stepanovs knew we were to arrive that day, but we had, given the unpredict-
ability of the trains, planned to meet them at their home, the address of
which a Czech friend had transcribed into Cyrillic. I was clutching that
unhelpful scrap of paper when a man pulled up beside us in an old Lada,
speaking rapidly, incomprehensibly and encouraging us to get in. A taxi,
perhaps? A serial killer? Hesitantly I showed him the slip of paper, which
he studied for a moment, and then he began nodding, vigorously, and we,
tepidly, climbed inside. Ten minutes later I paid him a few US dollars,
which pleased him greatly, and we found ourselves at the Stepanovs' door.

By evening, we were fast friends. We thought of Polo and the Khan,
how their exchange had to begin with ambiguous gestures and signs to
cross the void of language, but in our case, vodka seemed to function
remarkably well as a translator, and before long we were talking, I'm fairly
certain, about their daughter, Anna, and son-in-law Tolya, and how they
were adapting to American life. Leonid, the father, told us about his past
career as a radio journalist and how, with a famous voice, he'd performed
public readings of the great Russian poets to audiences of thousands, but
with the empire crumbling he was now plying his trade as a nine-fingered
carpenter. As our energy sagged and finding more to say became a challenge, he softly switched to Pushkin and we sank into the night listening
to his resonant, rhyming voice. Come sober, cat-tongued morning, we were
from different worlds again and it took three props and a demonstration
for us to understand we were being asked if we wanted milk in our tea.

Once that was settled, they drove us through Kaliningrad City, which
forty-five years after the War remained a shell of a city with bombed-out
ruins sprinkled between their soulless, efficient replacements. Of the deeper
past, one of the few remnants was the grand Kaliningrad Cathedral, whose
shadow covers Immanuel Kant's grave. In the afternoon, we drove out of
town to their dacha, a simple cabin near a small village. We went mushroom-
ing in the woods, then Mila cooked our find in a peppered heavy cream,
which we ate over thick slices of black bread. Throughout the day, a steady
stream of friends stopped by to inspect the American visitors, greeting us

with gestures and toasts. One was a former Soviet army officer who had been stationed in Prague in the 1970s, and there was a momentary expectation that he and I might actually speak before we realized that we were simply two sides of an imperialist coin spinning on a map, and neither of us had bothered to learn, neither had needed to learn, more than the basics of Czech.

As the sun went down, most of the village had found its way to the Stepanovs' cottage. Engorged by the full moon and two Americans to entertain, the men were in a spirited mood, pouring one another goblet shots of vodka, which we'd chase down with sour pickles and bitter green onions. After a long, nagging suspicion, I confirmed that the guy with the guitar was playing Bob Dylan songs. Later a couple of men returned, though I'd been oblivious to their departure, carrying heavy loads wrapped in waxed canvas, which they laid before the rest of us and began to unroll: a cache of rifles and shotguns, which to my bleary eyes looked as though they'd been buried since before the last World War. Then they started to hand the guns around between the men. I was given a heavy antique shotgun.

As Helena and a few other uninvited, suddenly sober women watched, we men—armed and liquored—loaded ourselves onto the back of a flat-bottom truck, three in the cab, and another dozen of us hanging on to the rails as we careened far off any road I could recognize, through fields and over small hills. Occasionally someone would holler, smack the roof of the cab, and the truck would come screeching to a halt, sending most of us half-tumbling to our knees, while someone fired off a shot at some imaginary prey. When we finally stopped for good, it was at the entry to a large field, covered in some kind of wild daisy that grew above my waist, echoing the moonlight. One of the more exuberant guides explained by pointing two fingers at his eyes, then pulling them back out and toward the field. He hooked his fingers like rough tusks jutting up from his lower jaws and snorted, then raised a phantom gun and pulled the trigger. I understood perfectly: when you see the wild boar, shoot it.

As someone raised on a steady dose of Asterix comics, and as someone whose inhibitions were thoroughly pickled, the idea of hunting—and ultimately roasting and devouring—wild boar was a dream come true. What

I didn't understand was why we needed to split up, armed and in the dark. But there was no arguing. For good measure, they stuck me with a hulking, blacksmith of a man, Kolya, who led me out into the daisies. I kept thinking this was all a bad idea but as in a dream, I followed the flow of events. As we went deeper, creeping through the weeds with the drunken delusion of subtlety, we could occasionally hear a companion cursing or singing until he was shouted down by the rest. Every once in a while, a thunderous shot would rip through the night and Kolya would duck and I would tumble behind him, followed by a fury of calls, confirming that everyone was alive and that the devious boar had miraculously escaped our clutches. After trudging a mile or so and repeating this charade a handful of times (any life-loving bovine had long since crossed the border), the allure of another drink trumped our bloodthirst, and we turned back, regathering at the truck to clink bottles and relay how close, how very close we'd come to killing that delicious beast. When I stumbled back to the cottage, Helena was asleep with her nose to the wall.

There was no walking on to Lithuania, not with hosts such as these who showered us with generosity while continually insisting that we'd be robbed, raped, and murdered in no time flat if they left our sides. On the day of our departure, a handful of our new friends gathered, and in a caravan they drove us north to the border, stopping along the way to pick wild mushrooms, which they added to a package they'd prepared for us of sausages, heavy bread, cucumbers, and vodka, which fed us for several days. When we finally said farewell, it was with many promises that we'd meet again, perhaps in America, which eventually we did.

For the next few days, we inched up the Lithuanian coast, our progress slowed by a cold rain that seemed like it might continue until the end of time. Perhaps it was simply because of our ties to Anna and Tolya, but we'd been overwhelmed by the warm embrace of nearly all the Russians we'd met. The Lithuanians, however, were another breed, clearly distrustful of two American backpackers off the beaten trail; their pubs, at least when we disturbed them, were unnaturally quiet. We would invariably find some place to stay, often a room in a home—which might, for example, have the appearance of a western home but no plumbing—than in a non-existent hotel, but even there our hosts kept a distance between us.

The sadness of those places began to wear on us as well, or perhaps it was simply being midway on a journey when the days get long and you no longer have the thrill of beginnings, the satisfaction of arrival. There's a line from Jack Gilbert, something about how the heart never fits the journey because one always ends first. On top of it all, everything we owned was soaked through; everything we saw was filtered through sheets of rain.

"I'm starting to think of it as a kind of animal," I said, probably just to break the silence that had settled around our lunch like another serving of cabbage, reaching into myself and hoping to find something clever, "something tracking us down. This rain picked up our scent out of Gdansk and has been on our trail ever since. And now here we are, two rabbits hiding in this pub, but the rain knows it has us cornered, that sooner or later we'll have to come out."

"I was thinking of it differently," Helena eventually said, just when I'd begun to suspect she was ignoring me altogether, "how rain makes everyone, everything else carry it. It soaks into our bags, our shoes, our hair; it fills every crack and hole. In its view each of us is just another little emptiness for it to fill."

After a while, she continued: "If you could change one thing about yourself, what would it be?" Perhaps she too was simply trying to keep a conversation going, but I sensed she was ready for me to become someone else.

Facing a trap, I felt myself immediately recoil. I knew that there are true answers—that I would like to write with the cool, detached brilliance of Jorge Luis Borges rather than with the overblown self-dramatization of a twenty-four-year-old adolescent. I knew that there are correct answers— that I wanted to be a more honest, open person, both with myself and with Helena. That I wanted to be more present. But because I felt cornered, because my shoes were full of rain, I decided to give the wrong one. "My hands," I eventually said. "I hate how sweaty they can get. If I could change one thing about myself, I'd love to have dry palms. What about you?" We finished our meal in silence.

While trying to work up the willpower to get back on the march, a boisterous man plopped himself down at our table—utterly indifferent to or perhaps attracted by the tension between us—and launched into us in fearlessly mangled English. "Hey man, what the fuck here you doing, you are crazy, beautiful kids?" he roared. We did our best to explain, hiking along the coast, ultimately up to Tallinn. He thought that was hilarious and without question the dumbest thing he'd ever heard. Assuring us that there was nothing worth seeing for many, many miles ahead but peasants, mosquitos, and misery, he told us he would drive us north to Palanga, where we could stay with his mother until we were ready to push on. It seemed a bit of a violation of our ambitions, but we'd already started to cheat, and with the rain continuing to fall, we said that would be great.

Of course Ondrej drove recklessly, with great flair and a disdain for concentration. He was consumed by a kind of manic energy and spoke for almost the entire ride. He had a quality I have always envied of being able to express himself in any language, grammar and vocabulary be damned, simply because of his compulsive need to make himself heard. He was in a bad way, we quickly learned, because his wife had found out about his mistress and was furious, and now his mistress had figured out that he wasn't really going to leave his wife, unless his wife kicked him out, in which case he might, but in the meantime his mistress had told him to get lost, and then there were the kids. Or something like that. I was charmed, but Helena half-expected he would murder us, especially when he turned off the main road, without any explanation, without a pause in the narration, and rocketed down a narrowing gravel strip and into a ravine where he came to an unexpected stop. Fortunately he just needed to pick flowers for his mother.

When we finally arrived at her place, it was nearing dusk and he made a flamboyant entrance inspired no doubt by any number of b-roll Italian movies, shouting out, "Mama! Mama!" and waving his bouquet. She was thoroughly unimpressed and un-Italian, a grey-haired, elderly lady with wide, swollen ankles sitting in an upholstered chair that had succumbed to generations of babushkas. He introduced us, explained our trip and that we were young people in love and would be staying with her for a few days. She nodded, ever so slowly and gravely. Clearly we were not the first unexpected, unneeded guests he'd brought home, and we began to feel deeply uncomfortable.

"Perhaps..." I offered.

"Nonsense!" he declared. "Everything is fine."

Then they began to speak in rapid, untranslated clips, and he in turn became more somber.

That morning her dog had given birth to a litter of puppies, and she'd been waiting all day for Ondrej's arrival so he could drown them, something he clearly had no desire to do. In his desperation he suggested instead that he put them out in a crate for neighbors to take, or that he drive them out to some farm, or maybe we should just wait a couple of days to see what happened. But she was unmoved. Every solution crashed against her unflinching solemnity, against the necessity of their death. Finally he relented, but in an inspired final maneuver insisted that he first needed to care for his guests, so leaving our bags in the hall, he shepherded us back into his car and took us to the local pub, where we bought him rounds of drinks and we all told stories about the dogs that had accompanied us through childhood and had been, at one time or another, our closest and most loyal friends. To my surprise and his relief, Helena held his hand. Finally he said it was time, and we all drove back to his mother's, but instead of getting out with the two of us to complete his murderous, filial assignment, Ondrej gave us a little wave and drove off into the night, to his mistress or wife we never learned. If our bags had not been inside the house, we surely would have disappeared too, but we had nowhere to go but in. We knocked on the door and she answered, looking disappointed but not the least bit surprised that her son had absconded, leaving her with two additional puppies.

* * *

We'd been traveling for weeks, often by foot then bus, sometimes in a stranger's car. We'd seen small, indistinguishable towns of Soviet bloc housing and light cedar forests. Glimpses now and then of the Baltic Sea, and then an afternoon on a deserted beach, the sun surprisingly sharp through a Soviet-sized ozone hole. There had been days when we felt completely connected and others when we each felt bound to an impossible stranger. Each day we went a little farther north; it was midsummer, and the sun barely dipped before rising again. The symbolism didn't escape us—we were supposed to arrive at a point of clarity about our future together, free of darkness, but the light was mostly blinding, exhausting. The real issues are simpler—how to clean our clothes, or where, in the height of summer, could a green vegetable be found?

Occasionally someone else would enter our little world for a moment, but mostly it was just us, and so the same conversation could continue over days, with long breaks and diversions, but continually circling back to the same themes, the increasingly entrenched positions. This morning we'd been negotiating the point of travel. Was it always a pilgrimage of sorts, a stripping away of the non-essentials, a process of finally becoming the person who could actually arrive somewhere, or was that just a mask for the far more trivial indulgence of accumulating incidents, funny stories to adorn one's persona? Did traveling make us lighter or heavier?

"Do you think we are imitating Marco Polo and Kublai Khan," I finally asked. "Two inhabitants of a world so vast, who've met on the great steppe, filling our days with fantastic dreams of all the places we have seen and will visit, so overwhelmed by their abundance that they have to be described in symbols and abstractions?"

"Or," she continued for me, "are we more like Polo and Rustichello? Two lost souls, locked together in a single cell, perhaps for another week, perhaps until the end of our days, with nothing more to do than endlessly rehash the past, trying to turn it into some magical story?"

By the opposite end of day we were sprawled sleeplessly across a hostel bed, the midnight sun filling the room. We'd reached Tallinn, the last stop on this trip together, and soon there would be no place to go but backwards. Neither of us wanted to argue but we each felt the need to persuade the other of something important.

After a while I continued: "I think people can become someone else. Experiences are real, and they change us. Not overnight but over time—we see things, they affect us, we are transformed into something different from what we were."

She knew that I already knew the core of her reply, so there was no rush to get to it. Eventually she added: "Of course things happen, and of course we change, but these changes are like slipping into a new outfit, adopting a new style, picking up an accent. They're different but the differences are shallow and fleeting; what we are we are for better or for worse."

THE SPURIOUS GLAMOR OF CERTAIN VOIDS

When we returned to Prague there was a stack of mail Fisher had assembled for me in our apartment, the foreign stamps already delicately clipped as I'd taken too long and temptation had, once again, overwhelmed him. Among the handful of letters was a vintage postcard, a sepia-toned Prague streetscape of a closed doorway guarded by two bearded, stone-cut figures curling up the frame, their thick arms seeming to hold the weight of the building above them. On the back, in a practiced and impressive script, it read, "Colin, my friend, you are a Poet! Find me when you get back. Yours, Adam Y."

I'd been imagining versions of that postcard for some years, although in my fantasies it generally arrived in a richly embossed envelope with the seal of Farrar, Straus and Giroux in the corner, Knopf or Copper Canyon, or why not From the Posthumous Desk of Elizabeth Bishop or the living one of Charles Wright? And while I appreciated Adam's blunt enthusiasm, the letters I'd written in my own head, to my own self, generally stretched on a little longer, not just announcing that I was a poet but explaining why in elaborate, well-argued if slightly embarrassing detail.

I'd met Adam a little while back at Velryba, one of the many new bars that catered to the young Czechs who saw their future tilt west, as well as to the many Americans crowding the city, easily spotted by our notebooks and well-thumbed volumes of Kafka. In principle, we expats

were leery of one another, each too much a reflection of our true, moderate
selves, and our very proximity was a constant reminder that we had never
quite escaped America, just recreated a post-collegiate sliver of it over the
horizon, but that didn't stop us from joining rank too many nights in a
row for long bouts of cheap booze or, more rarely, a drunken roll. In ret-
rospect, it may be true that we were short on artistic talent, but there was
a genuine abundance of character, like my scoundrel roommate Arjun.
I'd first encountered him at another bar where he arrived drunk in the
late afternoon, stumbling and armed with four roses, moving loudly and
indelicately between the crowded tables, ensuring that all eyes were upon
him as he awarded his roses to the four loveliest women he could see, clearly
favoring those who were sitting with men uniformly taller but less dashing
than Arjun himself. And then he saw Lucia, who was sitting beside me,
and realized he'd made a mistake. For a naked moment he was lost, but he
quickly devised a solution, backpedaling through the room to one of his
previous stops where he, with profound apologies and circuitous explana-
tions, reclaimed his rose.

He had a copy of Robert Hughes' *Nothing If Not Critical* tucked under
his arm, and as he settled himself uninvited beside us it slid onto our table,
an unavoidable prop and Lucia took his flower and the trap. He immediately launched into Hughes' story of Sigismondo Pandolfo Malatesta, more
easily remembered as the Duke of Rimini, who, despite writing poetry
and being perhaps the most discerning art patron of his day, was excom-
municated by the Pope and canonized into Hell after sodomizing a papal
emissary before a cheering army. Arjun paused to confirm it was the same
word in Czech. His point, and Hughes' as well, was that art isn't necessarily
about making us better people. He then tried, unsuccessfully, to kiss Lucia.

He pulled a similar routine the first night he met Helena, agreeing to
meet us for a drink with his girlfriend, Katka, and arriving instead with
both Katka and another equally attractive young woman. Eventually the
five of us set off for The New D Club, where the Nigerian exchange students went to dance, but on the crowded street we lost Arjun and his new
friend, or more obviously they'd lost us. At the club, we tried to console

Katka who was first worried, and then—as time and drinks passed on and on—pissed. Finally, a good hour later, he burst (his preferred mode of entry) back into our sphere, shouting, "Katka, where have you been? I've been looking all over for you! Why did you desert me?" It was such a ridiculous, bald-faced lie that he stunned us all into submission yet again.

Adam had a wide cheeked, firm breasted, and perpetually disheveled Czech girlfriend, Nina, which gave him immediate cache in my eyes. On top of that, everyone knew who he was because when he'd arrived a few months ago with his partner, Scot with one T, a trust fund kid, they let it be known they were setting up a new press that would present expat writing and young Eastern Europeans in translation. That got our attention. Adam was a recognizable figure around town with his ginger hair and the flannel shirts he wore buttoned to the wrist and neck, even on the hottest days, with tufts of his mighty chest hair climbing like ivy over his collar. A southerner, he favored Flannery O'Conner and *A Confederacy of Dunces*. When Adam asked if he could read my manuscript, I did my best to keep my cool amid the swirl of ecstatic fantasies of world conquest and self-loathing that were cascading down through my intestines.

I spent the next several days ruthlessly editing my poems, which read so differently knowing an editor would see them next. I changed "grey" for "ashen" and then changed it back again; I cut out the weak before realizing I had misunderstood everything about myself, brought them back and cut out the rest. Finally, I had to get it out of my nervous hands before I ruined the whole batch. A few weeks passed and we bumped into each other every few days, with Adam apologizing that he hadn't had time to open it yet and then making an excuse why he needed to be somewhere else immediately. I was sure he had read it and could no longer even bear to be in my presence; I pretty much felt the same way. Then Helena and I headed north.

* * *

By the time I tracked Adam down a few days later, the future was starting to assemble itself with a reassuring clarity. They'd publish my book, *The*

Spurious Glamor of Certain Voids, which though obscure would become a kind of cult classic, passed like a secret word of initiation between true poets, a work that would make all of those who had stayed behind to attend MFA programs in tame American cities tremble. There would be whispers about me coming home. Though I'd still be unknown to virtually everyone, I'd have a little halo above me, a kind of glowing destiny. With a second book of poems a couple years later, this time with a leading American press, a prize or two, the waves would part. And perhaps the third book wouldn't be poetry at all, but something strange like *Invisible Cities*; in fact, as I imagined it, it *was Invisible Cities*. And after I'd written that, perhaps I'd write Borges' *Labyrinths*, and then back to poetry, but this time I'd write Anne Carson's *Glass, Irony and God*. Everything I wrote would be just a little off center, never a best seller, never one for the masses, but each a secret classic, each assembling its cult of true believers. By then I'd be teaching at a university, but I'd also be making so much money writing travel pieces and profiles for *The New Yorker* that I could walk away from it all and simply Be, whatever that meant.

"The poems you sent, there's really terrific stuff in there," Adam said at last, having made we wait through our first round of beers while he monologued about some troubles he and Nina were having, which included a burning rash.

"You think so? That's the last two years of my life, molested into words. I feel like it's finally starting to come together."

"So do I, so do I. Listen, this is what I'm thinking. Scot and I want to launch our press with a book of four new American voices from Prague, and we'd love to be able to include you."

I took a long, slow draw on my drink, hoping to give Adam the impression that I was overwhelmed by the wonderfulness of his news. "Four?" I said without conviction. "That's phenomenal. Who else are you thinking of?"

"We've got Kate Baldus, Gronke and Geoffrey of course. You're the missing piece, my friend. We've been waiting for you to come back to close the square. You know all of them, right?"

"Yes," I said, "yes, I know them." I couldn't really bring myself to say anything poisonous about Kate or Alex; in fact, in another circumstance, I might even have said something nice. But Geoffrey, Geoffrey with a G. How I loathed him and his gaunt face, that fraudulent name, that unbearable hair.

We'd been circling around one another for several years, having arrived in Prague in the same wave. He was, at first, someone I'd sometimes glimpse at the far end of a bar, a café or crossing the other way on the Bridge, like an unexpected face in the mirror. After a while we'd sometimes nod. I picked up bits and pieces about him—that he was from San Francisco, a writer, that he was with this or that woman or maybe both, that his Czech was nearly fluent.

One afternoon I was having a drink with an Irish woman who taught at my school. We were sitting at a bar window, our knuckles nearly brushing, when he passed before us along the other side of the street, and she gave a laugh, a little, nervous laugh, and turned scarlet red. I didn't really want to know, but I couldn't resist asking, "Do you know him?"

"Well," she said, "kind of." They'd met a few months back and had spent a day together wandering through Prague's many alleys and winding streets, drinking and joking, becoming tipsier and more flirtatious until they finally found themselves, by his design, up in the park on Petrin Hill. She thought he would try to kiss her, but instead, leaning in, he challenged her to a game: they'd stand on opposite sides of a large tree and masturbate—the winner would be the one to come first. "It was a tie," she added.

Not so long after, Geoffrey and I ended up at a long table together at Rubin, a little basement student bar under the Castle. There were others there too, maybe a dozen, mostly women, which of course made the notion of being right far more significant than it might otherwise have been. And there was wine, cheap, tooth-staining Moravian wine. Inevitably someone mentioned *The Trial*, which was the opening he'd been waiting for. Geoffrey informed us that Kafka had written a fundamentally political book. That what Kafka describes is a ruthless, absurdist bureaucracy that without cause subjugates an Any Man to its humiliating whims and arcane, incomprehensible procedures. The horror of Kafka's world is that this terrible oppression has become so normalized it barely causes a ripple; no one beyond Josef K himself seems the least bit surprised by the accusations or impossible demands placed upon the accused. Under such an oppressive system, all human relationships are corrupted, alienating us from each other and ultimately ourselves.

Although I was certain Geoffrey was intelligent, I suspected he had the kind of mind that was always right but never surprising, almost as though he were reading from a script of correct answers. (Borges, who was wrong about so many things but always in the most idiosyncratic and inventive of ways, was my patron saint.)

I felt, therefore, a need to correct him. The troubling part of the book, I assured him, wasn't the political overtones. Everyone, after all, knows that the State is inhuman. There is nothing remarkable about its menacing actions, and there are countless other books that document them. What gives *The Trial* its singular power is Josef K's reaction, his inability to assert his own innocence. Even though no crime is ever specified, no real charge ever brought forward, Josef K can't escape the nagging suspicion that it is true: he is guilty. Of something! The State is not some monstrous bureaucracy, but rather a projection of that part of the self that knows—deep down and inescapably—that we are bad. It tells us we have gone wrong and offers no correction other than punishment. What ultimately crushes Josef K is not his tormentors but his own terrible knowledge, despite any evidence or even charge, that they are right and that we deserve the impossible trials imposed upon us.

This went on for a while. We each failed to convince the other, and as for the others, they looked increasingly bored and drifted off into other conversations.

It surprised me, of course, when I, still fuming, tracked down a copy later that week and re-read *The Trial*, to realize that my interpretation was entirely wrong. Over and over again, despite what I remembered or had imagined reading, Josef K declaims his innocence. He isn't mortified by the horrible rightness of the judgement but rather by its absurdity;

although he submits to the Law, he does so because it is immoveable and he is exhausted. That didn't, however, make me any more sympathetic to Geoffrey.

"Just a thought," I suggested helpfully to Adam. "Maybe you should ax the hairboy? Figuratively or literally, whatever. Don't you think it's all smoke and mirrors with that guy?"

"Geoffrey? Are you kidding? His poems are amazing. And his fiction too. Did you hear he's got a story coming out with *Granta*?" I hadn't. "Now, the deal is that because of the economics we've got to keep this pretty light, which means we'll need to keep each of your sections to about twenty to twenty-five pages max. Let's say twenty. What I wanted to talk to you about is a few ideas on how we might get there from the full manuscript you sent."

"I'm honored, Adam. Really, this is great," the last word only half out of my mouth before another swig of beer washed everything else back down.

"It is, you idiot," Helena reminded me when I got back. "It's a book. Who cares if there are four of you, and who cares if Geoffrey is squeezed in there too? I'm sure they are all terrified that you'll make them look bad. It's what you've wanted, or at least a step closer than you've ever come before, right? This isn't the end, just where it begins."

She had a point.

Over the fall Adam and I went back and forth on which poems to include, cutting them out, putting them back, replacing them with newer work, then cutting those out, me playing poet, Adam playing editor. Then at last, thankfully, it was out of my hands, off into production.

There was a story one of my dad's friends had told me back when I was in high school that kept surfacing at this time, a form of imparted wisdom I hadn't yet been able to use but which had, apparently, been lurking somewhere in my mind, waiting for this moment. Somewhat like myself, my dad welcomed friends who were a bit louder, more troublesome, more pot-stirring than he could ever be, and Jerry fit that mold—a mathematician who liked showing up at summer parties in his "Just Another Iowa Jewboy" t-shirt. Thickening his Brooklyn accent for the occasion, he would challenge stunned Midwestern men to foot races, taunting them when they had no idea whether he was serious or not.

One night after he'd scared most of our well-behaved neighbors away, Jerry told me about the one time he'd been happy. Apparently math is a particularly cruel profession in that most people who make a discovery of any note make it when they are young, when the brain is most nimble and able to exert itself athletically for weeks on end in pursuit of an elusive solution. You can still teach into your forties and beyond, but if you haven't made your mark by the end of your twenties or just a few years later, you almost certainly won't. It's not about accumulated wisdom. In his case, he had his epiphany while still in graduate school. The hot math problem at his time was the local Langlands conjectures. All the young, would-be geniuses at the University of Chicago were chasing it, Jerry included, by day and by night, over endless pots of coffee, driving themselves to exhaustion and sickness, and finally he just couldn't stand it any longer, abandoning all his papers and broken pencils for a long walk along Lake Michigan. Only when he'd managed to stop thinking about the conjectures and was able to watch the sparkling light across the little waves were the myriad pieces able to rearrange themselves in his head, and to his utter surprise he caught a glimpse of a different way to begin. He rushed back to his apartment, spent all night working and by morning he had it—the answer that everyone in his field had been desperately chasing.

Jerry wasn't the humblest of men, and his immediate impulse was to rush to his professor's office, to burst through the door waving his proof in his hands. Or why not start with his friends, those fellow students with whom he'd spent so many frustrated nights? With so many lives to ruin with his genius, it was hard to know where to begin. And so he just sat back for a minute, and then he had his second realization of the day. There was no rush.

He knew at least two things: the answer to the Langlands conjectures and that everyone else was going about it the wrong way, that no one else would answer this question anytime soon. With that cushion, he let his imagination wander ahead of the immediate present and see everything that was coming—he'd write up his analysis for publication; it would be a featured article in a major journal; universities would come calling; there would be prizes and cash; he'd have graduate students of his own and soon tenure. Those were all things he desperately wanted, and he no longer had to worry about getting them. They were his.

Suddenly freed of that sense of urgency, he sat on his proof, sent it nowhere, told no one. His friends could sense there as something different about him, but who would have guessed that this was it? He was the only person in the entire history of the world to be able to answer this singular question, obscure as it was. It made him happy and complete, and so long as he kept this knowledge to himself he could attend lectures and go for drinks and do everything that he always did but with a different kind of confidence that it was all going to work out. For once, women found him irresistible. He loved those days but also knew they wouldn't last indefinitely; perhaps in fact the best part of it was already fading. So eventually he sat down and wrote his paper, sealed it up and sent it off. Everything that he knew would happen next happened, and it was all wonderful, but never quite as good as those strange weeks when the path opened for him and only he could see it.

As I walked away from Adam's office, I thought—that is how I want to feel in the months ahead, a luxurious time as I passed into a future that had been waiting for me to arrive; a time when, at last, I knew I would reach my destination, my destiny, and could finally enjoy the journey. Mostly though, I just felt a kind of anxious dread. I was still changing so much then that even things I'd written just months before felt like they were written by someone else entirely, someone more naïve and clumsy. I couldn't bring myself to re-read the poems I'd included out of fear of what I would find, let alone what others would see.

At last it arrived, late in the winter. I stopped by the apartment that had become their office; it was stacked high with boxes of books, as Adam and Scot had boldly convinced themselves as well of their predetermined ascent. And in truth, it was beautifully made, finely printed and bound on thick, wholesome paper, in elegant, understated font. They looked immensely relieved, like proud parents. I hugged them both. "Thank you," I said genuinely. Within days, copies were circulating throughout town, or at least through a small town within the town, predictably re-sparking bottomless resentment about who was in, who was out. The four of us, suddenly an "us," did a large reading at a popular pub, where at least half the room felt they had just as much right to be on the stage and who can say they were wrong?

When the review came out in Prague's English language paper and I saw it was signed by Beth Clover, whose bi-sexual girlfriend I had once accidently tongued, my tremors of dread proved entirely justified. "All the self-important anguish of Rilke," she observed, "with none of the lyricism." And: "Hamilton seems to think that if he drops enough foreign names and exoticisms into his poems, they'll do the work of elevating the mundane reality of his life into something the rest of us should care about." Geoffrey, on the other hand, "astonishing."

By then, I had decided to leave Prague behind and return to the States. Three years had been not the blink of an eye it would likely become but a lifetime of sorts, and the publication of *New Voices in the Old World* was a capstone. I'd arrived with a backpack full of books, and now I could go home with one of my own, even if I had to share it. For all of its limitations, I knew this was a perfect storm of opportunity: I would have the air of a published poet, an exotically published poet at that, but the book itself, of a small edition, published abroad, would be virtually unattainable and its single print review lost in the dust heap of history. All that would really be known is that I'd published a book or been published in a book, two easily confused ideas. Soon enough, my new, enduring works would overwrite whatever little embarrassments this one might cause.

A few years after his first volume was published, Borges was known to beg them back from family and friends. He searched the used bookstores of Buenos Aires for any copies of it he could find. Which he'd then burn.

Part Three

LABYRINTHS

"Cleveland?" Adam said when I told him. "Really?" He was laughing uncertainly, wondering whether I was making a joke or had become one.

I had never been to Cleveland before, never even gave it much thought, but Helena had been accepted into a PhD program there; she was going and invited me to follow. While it passed as romantic, even heroic, to give up my European sojourn for the Rust Belt, I knew an equal truth was that the time had come for me to leave Prague and I had nowhere else to go; there was nothing for me in Iowa or Amherst, and other friends had moved on into graduate school, real jobs, or marriages. She found us an apartment on the ground floor of a collapsing house in Tremont, an old Ukrainian neighborhood in an oxbow of the Cuyahoga River—the river that had, to Cleveland's enduring shame, burned for three weeks in the 70s. To the east, just over the bridge, sat downtown, while to the south the river was bordered by steel mills whose chimneys continued to cough fire into the sky, quite beautifully, actually, if you could abstract the image from its poisonous reality. After three years in a proper city that had encircled a gothic town with an Art Nouveau one, then wrapped that again inside a socialist realist experiment, Cleveland's vast industrial wasteland, the empty six-lane boulevards connecting nowhere with nowhere, were as exotic as anything I'd known.

For a little while everything felt hyper-real, little nuances of place that in time would normalize but for a moment seemed to hold some essential key: the neo-Fascist sculptures on the bridge celebrating the Mass Man of Industrial Age, how kids would cross the street to avoid someone walking a dog rather than throwing themselves in its path. Everyone we met had an elaborate story, perfected through repetition, about how they were going to leave—for New York, Seattle, places that you just can't get to from Cleveland. From our permanently collapsing apartment, we'd sometimes go weeks unable to reach our landlord, who would occasionally need to go into hiding with his wife and stepdaughter when her ex-husband was reported to be on the loose.

Undoubtedly because someone else failed to show up (perhaps the one person to fulfill the fantasy of leaving Cleveland), in the late weeks of August I parlayed our book into an adjunct teaching job at Cleveland State University, where I felt incredibly grateful to make $800 a month. Until then, money had never been a major worry for me. I'd been raised in a comfortable family on the right side of a university town that pretended to be classless, in a slightly larger house than virtually all of my friends, and since I was fourteen I'd had odd jobs—taking tickets at the swimming pool in the heat of summer, delivering newspapers on frigid Iowa winter mornings, clearing restaurant tables then making pizzas—that had kept cash in my pockets. My grandparents had paid for college, and when my grandmother had died a few months before my graduation, I inherited $30,000, a transformative sum to a twenty-one-year-old, that had allowed me to live in the heart of old Prague rather than the ninth circle of socialist housing, and to make regular trips to Paris, side adventures to Turkey and the Baltics. But now it was virtually all spent.

In place of all that was a twelve-year-old, rust-bellied Toyota Tercel that Helena and I shared, so light that it ascended, just slightly, toward Canada at every one of Cleveland's many bumps. Luxury was a bowl of Bourbon Chicken at a Japanese carry-out. Others have it so much worse, I know; what I want to share is this creeping feeling of having gone wrong. Wasn't my trajectory elsewhere? I'd made it from Iowa to Amherst to one of the most iconic cities in Europe, only to have Cleveland splatter like a ripe, yellow bug across my speeding windshield.

After my parents' divorce, my mom moved back to Philadelphia, a city of immense self-satisfaction, and married a man whose grandfather is honored with a statue in front of the Natural History Museum. It was an easy drive from Cleveland and we'd often escape our bare kitchen for the comfort of her home. She'd make a fabulous dinner, we'd all drink a bit too much, talk about books and laugh. But once my guard was down, she'd offer to introduce me to the children of her friends who worked in advertising firms or as financial brokers. "It might be really interesting for you to talk to Bees," she would say, in a suddenly more serious tone. They all had prep school nicknames like that, which she would have joyfully mocked when she'd been an Iowan but now she could pronounce with a straight face; she'd re-joined the club. "His boss thinks the world of him. He's just wonderful."

When I was in Prague, it had been easy to imagine myself on the edge of the future, that the whole world was watching to see what would happen right exactly there, but Cleveland was Prague's antipode, trapped in a doomed past, forgotten, lost. Some people could blame their parents for having birthed them in Cleveland, for failing to have paved them a way out, but how was I to explain having moved there willingly? By choice? You are either climbing up or tumbling down the ladder, and if I hadn't scraped my way out of a lower place—Akron, Youngstown—to arrive there, the only explanation that made sense was that I had fallen. With an unpoetic thud.

There is a Jack Gilbert poem about Orpheus, the greatest poet of them all, descending into Hell to bring back his beloved, dead Eurydice, confident that his all-powerful song will protect him from whatever horrors he'll find, that his song will seduce Death, when he realizes—the demons have no ears. In house after house, I saw vast collections of CDs, but there was almost never a book, and I knew that people here found my poetic aspirations curious, a tad exotic perhaps in an archaic way, like wearing English bowler hats, but of no genuine interest.

A sense of failure began to permeate everything I did, including the books I read. In Cleveland, Denis Johnson, troubadour of humiliations, spoke to me. All his heroes were fuck ups and losers, evoking disgust not just in others but in themselves as well. He had become so alienated that when he holds himself on a cool spring night, he "finds himself in the arms

/ of a total stranger, / the arms of one he might move / away from on the dark playground."

Jorge Luis Borges had been among my most treasured authors since I'd first discovered him as a late adolescent, and I'd read his *Ficciones* and *Labyrinths* over and over. Although his stories rarely stretch on for more than a handful of pages, they are indifferent (as, in the end, I also am) to the terse, strained conversations between a man and a woman falling out of love and leap instead, for example, to massive conspiracies of intellectuals—poets, engineers, philosophers, linguists, historians—who are secretly creating an alternate world that is slowly consuming our own. And he'd made one of the great, liberating discoveries in literature, that there is no need to torture yourself writing long novels when instead you can churn out fake reviews—all the better if they are somewhat critical—of your unwritten works.

In one of these fictions, as he called them, Borges wrote: "It may be that universal history is the history of a handful of metaphors." I think he meant that as much as we like to celebrate the uniqueness of our individual experiences, history is little more than the repetition of stock characters and a few ideas that roll around in our minds like sand inside an oyster, occasionally spitting out a pearl, though remarkably like every other pearl strung around time's neck.

One of my favorite Borges stories is "The Lottery of Babylon," which describes an entire city that has become so addicted to the lottery that it must continually drive the stakes higher, until the lottery no longer dispenses money but destiny. To live in Babylon, which is to submit to its lottery, is to tumble through lives at the roll of the dice, and as a result individuals are stripped of their singular identities and histories. One day you are sleeping in a gutter, the next in a palace, not because you've changed in any essential way but because the lottery has reassigned you to another fate. Until the wheel spins again.

A similar vision of characters filled and emptied and filled again, churning through possible selves, is repeated in "The Immortals." A Roman soldier sets off in pursuit of a vague rumor of a distant city that holds the promise of immortal life. After a long journey that purges him of companions and hope, he crosses a thin, sickly stream—not the grand river that had been foretold—and enters a nightmarish ruin comprised of dead ends, unreachable windows, puzzles and other architectural decisions designed either by a madman or to make you one.

The ruins are uninhabited, but eventually beneath the city walls— outside of civilization—he finds a little tribe of semi-human "troglodytes." One of these half-men takes to trailing the Roman, who has lost the will to go any further, and the Roman disdainfully names him Argos. After time and a tremendous storm that seems to awaken him, the half-man finally responds, "Argos, Ulysses' dog." Stunned, the Roman asks him what he knows of the *Odyssey*, and the man replies, "Very little. Less than the poorest rhapsodist. It must be a thousand and one hundred years since I invented it." These men are, the Roman realizes, the Immortals, from whom time has washed identity, ambition, expression. While his first reaction is disbelief that such a miserable creature could ever have written the *Odyssey*, that such a creature *was* Homer, the Roman ultimately accepts that, "if we postulate an infinite period of time, with infinite circumstances and changes, the impossible thing is to not compose the *Odyssey*, at least once." If you keep scattering letters around long enough (and yes, it might take an eternity), they'll have no choice, eventually, but to assemble themselves into beautiful, enduring verse.

There was a time—especially when I was seated in a European café, and when I felt that my potential was boundless—when I found Borges thrilling, and to read him was to be exposed to an elegant, erudite imagination that was continually opening up new possibilities. But in Cleveland, in sad, self-loathing Cleveland, I was increasingly attuned to Borges' fundamentally nihilistic worldview. He returns repeatedly to just a few metaphors that mimic infinity but are always trapped in claustrophobic spaces: mirrors; a rigidly geometric, pleasureless library that contains every book that could ever be written in 410 pages using just twenty-two letters, periods, and commas; an infinite sphere whose center is everywhere and whose circumference is nowhere; labyrinths; the paralysis of infallible memories;

the pampas; a single point discovered under an innocuous flight of stairs, through which the entire universe can be viewed; blindness. Rather than passages into the infinite, these were each horribly closed, inescapable loops.

Through those Cleveland years, I wrote and I wrote. I wrote in the mornings, and I wrote between classes when I should have been correcting papers. I wrote in my mind while walking in endless circles through our neighborhood, and I wrote in our evenings while Helena studied. Sometimes I tried to write like Denis Johnson, and other times like Borges. And then another month it would be Gregor von Rezzori, sometimes like a Louise Glück flower. I wrote stories that were like poems, poems that were like stories, stories that were about poems, stories that pretended to be essays, travelogues about places I'd never been, outlines of novels I'd never write.

I started something I thought might be a novel about Harry Houdini, as he first masters the art of escape but ultimately realizes its curse—that everything he touches slips through his hands, his inability to remain present, connected to anything. And another about the Belgian King Leopold who rules the Congo, a private estate that dwarfs Europe, but which he has never visited himself, and how deep in his demented reign he starts to wonder if it even exists, and if not, who created that illusion and why.

Immersed for a few weeks in the stories of the Polish poet Zbigniew Herbert, I started something else called "The Hell of Insects," about a lethargic, mediocre 16th century Dutch student who, at the University in Leyden, should be studying mathematics, Latin, medicine, astronomy, the Oriental languages, but instead finds himself increasingly obsessed with the lowest of creatures, bugs. At a lecture, the professor had prepared a dung beetle for the students' inspection. It was turned on its back with its shell split open and pinned to the table. As he peered into the body, my hero did not see the foul, minute cavity the professor described, but a vast space, delicate and crafted. He felt as he'd been told to feel when gazing at the stars: swallowed in God's voice, humbled. From there, his descent is certain as he finds that what fascinates him, what brings him to life, is something that repulses virtually everyone else. And then the insects began to speak to him. That felt more like Cleveland than Kafka.

I'd come to know myself well enough to anticipate the pattern. It would always be a struggle to begin, trying to extract a few words from the great silent void, but eventually something would catch and the sentences would start rolling out, one after another, a few pages. Eventually the tips of my fingers where I pressed the pen would begin to ache a bit, and my mind would start to drift, almost always to fantasies of accomplishment and fame—how this time my masterpiece would be picked up by *The Atlantic* or *The New Yorker*, and then I could see myself, handsome and thoughtful, on the stage of the New York Public Library, a vast audience of rapt women and defeated men. But when it came to re-reading my latest soul squirt, it was as though a trick had been played and my brilliant creation had been swapped out for a poor imitation written by a sixteen-year-old: the ideas were the same, the words were the same, but what had been fluent, refined, and arresting came back clumsy and overwrought.

There is a poem by the Brazilian clerk Carlos Drummond de Andrade in which he attempts to create an elephant, a wild, redemptive dream. But it quickly becomes clear that his resources, some cotton, silk floss, feathers, and glue, are hopelessly unequal to the task: the elephant "also has tusks / of that pure white matter." What he is able to build is nothing more than a parody of nature's great beast. Still he sends his creation out into the world, but it is so monstrous that no one will even look at it. Although the elephant lumbers through town, he is so poorly made that when he finally returns home, it is with "his paws staggering, / crumbling in the dust." The glue has come unstuck, and all of his delicate crafting falls apart. (A brotherhood of poets who worked as clerks, that lost profession: Drummond de Andrade, Cavafy, Pessoa, T.S. Eliot, Whitman.)

There were, undoubtedly, all sorts of practical reasons why I was failing to break through—a lack of talent, a weakness for clichés, a tedious seriousness which permeated my writing while avoiding the rest of my life—but the one I began to fixate on was my ability to sleep. When I'd lie down in the evening, it was rarely long before I could release myself into it, and if on occasion I woke during the night, it was almost a pleasure to lie still and half-lucid in the dark, my lids sinking further down with every soft exhale, pushing away whatever thought had hoped to hold me. Sweet oblivion. Sweet indeed, but I suspected that if I were a true artist, I'd be wrestling against it, my mind so relentlessly alert, so obsessively on the track of understanding that each night would be a kind of hell.

That's how it had been for Borges, who'd been afflicted with insomnia from early childhood. While the fit slept, Borges would lie—hour after miserable hour—in the dark classifying mythological beasts by the virtues of the heroes who conquered them and inventing nounless languages. Like a golden thread, these thoughts lured him beyond rest into a knotted, thorny labyrinth where the more exhausted one becomes, the more unattainable sleep is.

In his bottomless nights, he took some comfort pitting his insomnia against the numbness of minds that passed uneventfully from waking to sleep as though there were no real difference between them. An admirer of knife-fighters, insomnia was Borges' heroism: like being condemned not for lust or greed, but for defying God. And just as some men forged their strongest friendships on soccer fields at noon or riding across the sun-seared Pampas, in the ink-black hours Borges read and reread the authors who came to be his true companions: Chesterton, Dante, Schopenhauer, De Quincey, Kafka, Wells, Stevenson.

Perhaps to punish him for going where I couldn't follow, I started a story about Borges late in his days, after a lifetime of eternal nights, suddenly finding himself losing his insomnia. Although he knows he should welcome sleep as a gift—perhaps a reward for all his achievement—he imagines it instead as an animal, sleek and lethal, which has picked up his scent. As a child, he had judged each encyclopedia by the quality of its tiger engraving, and he was haunted by the tiger's elegant pacing at the Buenos Aires zoo. For half a life, he had written about tigers and perhaps, it occurs to him now, each poem or story was another cage, somehow keeping the tiger safely enclosed. But the cage is broken, the tiger set free. From his bed, he can sense the ruthless cat's approach.

He is being ridiculous, melodramatic, he knows. He reminds himself that sleeplessness was hell. How little of the night was actually spent ceiling-staring as his mind conjured apocrypha? In the darkest hours, he was too tired to think, or to think anything clever. He forgot the Icelandic sagas and remembered his back, which ached, and the women who wrote him long but passionless letters. His body smothered his mind: he could feel it in conflict with everything it touched: the hot sheets, starlight, a nonexistent crumb. In a last fit of will, he'd escape exhaustion into a kind of impotent rage—to be choked in flesh, like being buried alive. And when that passed, he was just a prematurely old, priggish man alone in the dark, waiting for the dawn.

Nevertheless, when he feels sleep's whispers brush his sheets, he tries to stir himself by naming all the things he failed to see today that were visible to him only one week before: the half-circle inside an "e," the gap between Matilda's teeth when she scowls, salt on a boiled egg. But rather than fend off the dreamtiger, the rhythm of loss draws her closer. *My best work is behind me*, he thinks as she sinks her teeth into the nape of his neck. *The effort has blinded me and left me mortally tired.* This charge is meant to jolt him from his slumbering, but more resigned than scared, he lies perfectly still in sleep's motherly jaws.

* * *

The highlight of my days was checking the mail. I was sending out poems and essays to magazines and contests all across the country. Despite consistent evidence to the contrary, I was able to persuade myself time after time that this message in a bottle would rescue me from obscurity, triggering the long-delayed but destined ascension. Each submission was packaged with a self-addressed stamped envelope that would—sometimes after just a couple weeks, but more often half a year or a full natal term—appear in my mailbox like a letter to myself. How thin they were, how short on news. Generally there would be nothing more enclosed than a pre-printed rejection note. I felt so grateful when an intern would scribble a few words at the bottom: "Nice work!" "Really interesting!" I reminded myself that David Markson's *Wittgenstein's Mistress* was rejected fifty-four times, including by eight publishers who called it "Brilliant!" And then once or twice a year some wonderful little journal, so remote that I'd never even seen a copy of it, would accept a poem or two, and I could believe again that I would achieve everything I had foreseen so long ago.

Over-celebrating one such minor victory, Helena and I drove to a big-box shop that was one of the last places in Cleveland to actually sell books, although its entire ground floor had already been repurposed for music and movies. At the top of the stairs, there were several tables where the newest, most promising titles were on display at thirty percent off. I was moving, as usual, past them when I saw Geoffrey's novel. I wasn't entirely surprised, I suppose: I knew it existed, that it was being reviewed, that the reviews—the kind that invariably included his author photo—were energized and hopeful. He'd written about Prague, about this curious moment when a swarm of jaded, purposeless Americans had re-attached themselves to history. It was, apparently, cruel and very funny. I shouldn't have been surprised at all, but for some reason—self-delusion, protection—I'd failed to believe it was quite real.

I paused beside it and read the over-the-top blurbs, then bent the pages back and let them flip past my thumb. I suppose I half-expected my name to come leaping out but everything went by in a blur. Then I set it back down and continued on my way to the lonely poetry section, a generous three columns I had cruised so many times I felt I could repeat it from Ai to Zukofsky. That day, however, a different spine caught my eye, four of them actually, a handsome sequence of books published by Wesleyan University Press by a poet I had never heard of and whom, to my regret, I can no longer remember. What I do remember was a horrible sinking feeling that this anonymous person had achieved so much—four books with Wesleyan—and I, one of the small cult of poetry readers, had never even heard of her. I felt terribly sad—for her, for myself, for our doomed tribe.

Not so long after that, I was struck by lightning. At the mailbox, one of my envelopes returned just a little thicker than usual, and when I ripped it open I found a genuine letter from the kind editors at the Kent State University Press informing me that I'd won their annual prize for Ohio poets, and that they'd publish my chapbook, *The Last Voyage of the Beagle*, the following year. In a grand twenty-three pages, it purported to be excerpts of the diaries of a doctor, David Mountolive, who had travelled aboard Darwin's great expedition. Although rarely mentioned by Darwin, Mountolive was part of the crew that helped determine the longitude of Rio de Janeiro, watched Argentine gauchos bola down ostriches, and discovered, at Punta Alta, a gigantic fossilized rhinoceros whose bones, Darwin wrote, "tell their story of former times with almost a living tongue." Mountolive watched, first with curiosity then growing discomfort, Darwin note the slight variations in the beaks of mockingbirds across the southern seas.

While these discoveries would ultimately allow Darwin to unearth a revolutionary truth, the crews' conversations and debates led Mountolive to a conclusion more in line with their times: "I've come increasingly to suspect that God assigned the task of creation to his most poetic angels, rather than those with a basic knowledge of engineering." Pursuing this theme over the long, and at times spectacularly dull five-year, round-the-world voyage, Mountolive, in the privacy of his journal, in the boredom of his nights, gave himself license to become that angel himself and recount how our world came to be. I hadn't quite managed to expel Rilke from my poetry.

I gave a well-attended reading at Kent State and invited many of the people we'd met in Cleveland—Sean and Mary Margaret, Lee Mars, Irene and Tom, Angie, a few students. I was flattered by how many made the trip down to attend, by how much they enjoyed it—perhaps just the oddity of it—or at least convincingly claimed they did. Several generously said some version of, "I don't know anything about poetry but I think yours is great." I got a fine review in the campus paper, as well as an unusually flattering and remarkably large photo. I sent copies, of course, to all my friends and extended family; very few commented on the poems themselves but many sent kind notes about how happy I must be. It eventually sold about a hundred copies.

THE SAVAGE DETECTIVES

Precocious Arthur Rimbaud won all the school prizes in his provincial French village, and while just an adolescent he began to write brilliant poems; one he penned at fifteen continues to be anthologized more than one hundred years after his death. Of course little Charlesville, its priests and Catholic school, could never hold him. It was only a matter of time until he escaped. His first run failed with Rimbaud imprisoned for vagrancy almost as soon as he deboarded his train in Paris, but he was clever enough to quickly find the help he needed—a one-way ticket to the capital of the world sent from the easily overwrought poet Paul Verlaine, who'd been moved by a letter from Rimbaud. And thus began a reign of terror upon the Parisian avant-garde.

To write visionary poems, the world's worst house guest demanded a "derangement of the senses," and this dirty cherub drowned himself in absinth, corrupted desperate men, fed his scalp to lice. Everyone around him went a little mad, Verlaine most of all. Although Rimbaud called his poems "illuminations" and aspired to become a seer, his world became even darker and more blinding. After two electric years, they'd had enough of his variety of genius. Fists were waved in his face. His only friend shot him. Those who'd been scandalized by his early provocations learned to ignore them. And then the worst humiliation: the little anarchist had to be rescued from the pit he'd dug by his moralizing mother—the "Mouth of Darkness," as he called her—who hauled him home by the ear for a good scrubbing.

By nineteen, his life as a poet was over.

Many poets, and especially those who find no path to an audience, give it up, eventually drifting into other lives as teachers, restaurateurs, accountants, novelists, and car dealers, but it is hard to think of anyone who took as strange a path as Rimbaud. After recovering at his mother's and begging a few coins from her, he traveled to Germany, to Java. When he left, there was no one to see him off or even notice the departure. Not a single poem—his immortal, immoral outbursts—made the journey. His journey was to purge all that. Eventually he found his way to the Red Sea town of Harrar where he began a second life bartering coffee, ivory, and guns. Years passed.

When the Devil finally had the nerve to visit Rimbaud, He took the form of Alfred Sterling, a smug English trader. By then, Rimbaud had lost most of his hair, learned to speak a dozen languages native to the markets of the world, and squirreled away a small fortune he wouldn't live to spend. The cancer that ultimately killed him was already devouring his leg.

Sterling had just returned from Europe with his fresh cargo of goods when he and Rimbaud shared the awkward greeting of friends who hadn't seen each other in months and who never much liked each other in the first place. But that didn't stop Sterling. With a sly grin he told Rimbaud that on his voyage back from the continent he'd met a French journalist who begged him for tales of Wild Abyssinia. When Sterling obliged with stories of their rugged crew, the journalist was pleasantly amused until Sterling mentioned "Arthur Rimbaud," which caused the journalist to cough up his wine. Apparently a young man by that strange name had, a decade ago, savaged Paris with his vicious wit and vile tastes. And then disappeared. Now his poems were being re-discovered, and in his absence he'd become the hero of a new cult of poets. "Is it true?" Sterling laughed. "Are you, our most heartless merchant, a poet?"

Rimbaud had learned to remain expressionless at the most devastating news—that his partner had been murdered by bandits, that the king would embargo his goods. He was smarter than they were, and that meant he could generally find some profit in events; like any other commodity, a disaster can be traded. To calm himself, he thought about using his thumb to uproot Sterling's left eye.

"Somebody else," he answered.

In Harrar, Rimbaud avoided the other Europeans, Sterling and the rest. It wasn't hard to do: he was a difficult fellow, respected for his tough trading but not liked. Behind his shut door, he thought about how he went further—through his worst self and into this thorny world. The thought was meant to rejuvenate him, to justify the gloom of this shack, but he couldn't summon the conviction. He knew he was chased out of Europe like a stray from the kitchen. He tried to imagine what news could have shocked him, the unshockable Rimbaud, more than to have been discovered, to exist.

But it proved only one thing—the avant-garde was as ridiculous as he always suspected. He'd seen totem worship wherever he'd gone. As a boy, he claimed his poems gnawed on the bitter bones of life, but the bones he chewed were covered in fat: indulgent perversity, extremist rhetoric. Flowery language is no less flowery because the petals are rotting; it just thickens the scent. That readers had been seduced by the thrilling obscenity of his work was no different—only less profitable—than natives selling their goats and souls for a mass-produced string of beads. We'll give up so much for the illusion of meaning.

He stopped dreaming of Art and Her laurels a long time ago, but what exile doesn't, in the darkest hours, dream of home? This was Rimbaud's: to buy a farm near Charlesville, to attract a good wife, even if she'd have to be a little past her prime, perhaps a widow. He'd raise a son, educating him to torment priests and master numbers. His mother could visit if it taught her how wrong she was. Lying on his rough bed, his stomach sore from sour goat-milk, it was enough of paradise.

Rimbaud had survived the monotony of Ethiopia by choking off his pleasures, but alone in the dark, he allowed himself this: What if his poems were good? What if he'd ruined himself for something rather than for nothing? The cynic in him hears all the old, impotent sailors of the world crying in their rum for the girl—always a shepherdess, a milkmaid—they left behind only to realize that her love was true.

Because the cynic was coupled with a masochist, he couldn't stop himself from wondering what would happen if he were to return someday not to a sad, broken farm but to Paris itself? He had almost forgotten the cold touch of glass, let alone the taste of a bistro's barrel. If the next poets revered his work, *understood* it, there would be a place for him at the heads of their tables, surrounded in cafés. No longer the too young looker-on begging for a place. Poet and adventurer, Master of Markets, he'd make short work of the critics who'd turned up their noses at the little ruffian he'd once been.

What surprised him most was how little, after the initial thrill, this fantasy interested him. Of course revenge is nice, but whom would the joke really be on? To have been a poet was bad enough, but to become a fashion? One of those celebrated bores he'd always sought to ridicule and offend? Never. He'd made his escape. Now, he had other matters to deal with: Sterling. Freshly returned from Europe with a small fortune in goods and his stupid grin. Rimbaud pictured him strutting through the streets like a fat rooster just waiting to be plucked.

* * *

For years I've taken pleasure in this story of Rimbaud, more pleasure than I ever got from his actual poems—the vision of the exile being offered the crown and turning it down, walking away from it all.

After *The Last Voyage of the Beagle* came out, all sorts of things happened in my life, many of them quite wonderful but not really the kinds of things I want to write about in this story. I swallowed my pride and left the false, poverty-inducing comfort of adjunct teaching, commuting instead to a dreaded nine-to-five job doing communications work for a consumer advocacy group. To my utter surprise, I loved it. I loved the discipline of day, the sense of accomplishment, the purpose of it. I loved having colleagues who shared my burdens and little victories, who talked about the bad movies we all enjoyed. In time, that job led to another, working in the suburbs of politics by helping public agencies pass tax referenda. As a poet, I'd always known I had a certain style and gift for phrasing, but also suspected I ultimately had nothing to say; in my professional life, I discovered I could create clear, purposeful prose out of the jumbles that ran through other heads and that made me valuable to have around. When Helena finished her PhD, she took a job in Minneapolis—a city with bookshelves—and once again I followed and time rolled along. We had two boys, a dog, a house. We made friends. When we could, we traveled, though rarely back to those places we'd already been and supposedly knew, places that now belonged to another era, to another life, to somebody else.

With so much else crowding my days, I wrote less and less, and when I did, it was with more distraction than inspiration. I blamed Helena, of course, and then my kids and then my job from taking me away from my true, poetic self, but mostly what I felt was a kind of relief. The very best moments of writing had been extraordinary, but there were very few of those. More often I was caught in endless cycles of frustration at never being able to actually say what I really meant, always coming back to the gap between what I had envisioned, which was so alive and distinct, and what I ultimately produced, which was shallow. My elephants would stagger and collapse.

Perhaps the worst part was that people who knew something of my past would invariably ask if I was writing, always with a gentle tone as though they were expecting to touch a nerve, delicately trying to comfort me for the tragedy they hoped to tweak and experience for themselves. I learned to tell people I was a recovering writer. Day by day, with the grace of god, I stay off the stuff. They'd laugh and assume I was joking, but that's how it felt—a kind of low-grade sickness, an addiction, that more than anything else had become not a connection to the world but a barrier to it, a way of being alone. Occasionally when there would be a little void in life, a slow time at work, a birthday, I'd feel some temptation and maybe for a few days I'd fall off the wagon, buy a new notebook, a fancy pen. But it always passed, and generally without any sense of regret or loss.

And anyway, what is actually worse: to give up one's youthful dreams or to never grow beyond them?

* * *

"When I was a kid, three decades ago, the future was a long way off..." wrote Danny Hillis. As a child in the 1960s, he always knew that by "the future" people meant what happened after 2000. It was perfectly possible—perhaps even likely—that on January 1, 2000, we'd be served breakfast by robots, ride jetpacks to work, and wish our well-preserved parents on Mars a happy new millennium. With thirty-some glorious years before the future began, anything could happen.

But as the years and decades passed, most of these beautiful dreams failed to materialize. More tragically, we continued to hold out 2000 as The Future, and as the gap between today and tomorrow narrowed from decades to a single decade to just a few years, so too narrowed our ability to imagine a future much different from our present. We became increasingly focused on what could be achieved in a couple of years, or even a couple of quarters. Our aspirations contracted. And then we crossed over that border into a new era, but nothing rose up to replace 2000 as a horizon we were moving toward, as a repository of dreams. As a result, rather than working toward an aspirational horizon, we seem lost in a great void, lurching between apocalyptic visions of melting ice caps and murderously rational machines.

To reset our attention, Hillis designed the Clock of the Long Now, built to keep time for 10,000 years—a bit longer than the past history of human civilization. But rather than ticking every second like an anxious human heart, the Clock would tick just once a year acknowledging our collective solar orbit. All the mechanisms and materials would be designed to endure over millennia and withstand the unpredictable environmental changes of the earth; like its distant cousins the pyramids, the Clock of the Long Now is hidden in the desert.

"The past is too small for the future to inhabit," wrote Rem Koolhaas. An architect, Koolhaas foresaw the futility of our nostalgic bias for historic spaces—old cities, brick warehouses—in a human world growing exponentially. We may not like the idea of suburbs, high rises or new construction, but people need to live somewhere, and there is simply not enough of the past to cram us all into. To live only in historic spaces, or for that matter to live only in the past intellectually, is to suffocate. The math alone is undeniable, but how do we accept the future as something more than a consequence of living in the present? How does it become a nurturing environment rather than an inevitable void?

In one of Koolhaas's early proposals, back when he was more of a provocateur than a working architect, he came up with an ingenious, impossible solution. As the Chunnel was passing from dream to reality, ferry towns along both the English and continental coasts were threatened with irrelevance. As if to assert its existence, Zeebrugge, a modest Belgian town with grandiose delusions, proposed to build a massive sea terminal—with not just ferries but hotels, a casino, restaurants, and pleasures: all the infrastructure and amenities that would make the Chunnel, whatever its speed, look like no more than a death-trap hole in the ground.

Koolhaas submitted plans for the Zeebrugge Sea Terminal, and of course they were bold and iconic. But his real innovation was on the construction side. All the elements of this massive, two million-square-foot project could all be prefabricated in China, shipped around the world and then rapidly assembled in the waters off Zeebrugge. This strategy could beat the Chunnel's timeline, even if it meant a terrifying alien spacecraft materializing on the Belgian coast.

There was, Koolhaas noted, another way. The entire project could also be built on-site by just thirty-eight workers, all residents of Zeebrugge. The trade-off is that it would probably take them fifty to sixty years to complete, by which point the Chunnel itself might very well seem archaic. From the owners' perspective that probably seemed like an unacceptably long time, but from another perspective it might be exactly the right duration. Built slowly over decades by local workers, the Zeebrugge Sea Terminal would rise up not as a monstrous force but as an indistinguishable part of town and its heritage. By the time it was completed, most residents would know it as something that had always been a piece of their community—a place where their grandfathers and uncles had worked, where their mothers and fathers had met, where they had first dreamed of what might still be possible.

I found Hillis and Koolhaas while wandering the aisles of the Minneapolis Central Library, where I spent many breaks from work exploring unexpected shelves, clearly looking for something that would help me understand how I was moving through time, how with my horizons contracting I could still, at moments at least, reach beyond them to something more. But even though I enjoyed browsing the rows daily, memorizing the titles, I was losing my appetite to actually read. I still stacked books by my bed and used them to weight my shoulder bag, to make my desk look serious, but I found as many reasons to stop reading as there were books themselves—dissatisfaction with a voice, pace, a plot twist, a typeface. A single sentence, perhaps one I'd used myself, that I just couldn't forgive, without even knowing its crime. The ridiculous name of a main character. Restlessly I'd flip from one book to the next, rarely getting beyond a few chapters, never able to set up residence within it. Even worse, in these fallow reading periods everything else became just a little bit duller, washed out, colorless—as though what I had been absorbing from books I had been able to infuse into the rest of my life, and now I was living in its absence.

There were other pleasures, of course, simple ones like an afternoon stroll through our neighborhood of old Victorians, brick alleys and giant oaks, the kids running ahead armed with sticks with which they'd slash and gut imaginary foes. On this day, though, I already had a slight pain in my side as we set out, and before long I could feel it curling up under my ribs. I had to stop but it went right on, turning in a matter of minutes into a corkscrew twisting through my organs. Helena left me crumpled and gasping on the sidewalk with two terrified kids as she sprinted home for the car that would race us all to an emergency room. There it was obvious to everyone I had kidney stones (just like Montaigne, I thought once the pain subsided), even though nothing showed up on their scans. The stones, they assumed, must have passed, which I had a hard time accepting—wouldn't I know? But it was true that the pain subsided. When I was back again two nights later, after a three-am ambulance ride and I'd been thoroughly tubed, more tests revealed that it wasn't stones after all but that somehow I'd torn the inside of a vein, creating a small flap that, when I twisted and it flipped up, shut down the blood flow to one of my kidneys. The pain I felt was my organ dying inside me. Ultimately I lost about a half of my right one, though I suppose "lost" isn't exactly the word. I'm still carrying its dried husk around.

Having started to die a bit more actively, I felt like I was reconciling myself to my late thirties, but even that didn't prepare me for what came next. Like a much older man, I couldn't piss. At the library, over the urinal, I'd dribble out a little something while my swollen bladder, pulsating inside me, threatened to erupt; most of what I could produce was frightened sweat. Waves of this went on over several increasingly desperate weeks, cycling through multiple doctors who all agreed it was very curious for one so young to be having prostate troubles but had no better explanation. They suggested salt baths, laying off coffee, a toxic medicine that turned what little urine I could produce a shameful orange and stained all but the blackest pants. Finally a more invasive doctor realized there was expanding scar tissue from some past indiscretion choking off my urethra. He removed it, which perhaps saved my life but certainly not my dignity. A catheterized me lay in bed for two weeks, thinking that if this was thirty-eight, what was the point of even getting to forty, to fifty? If there had been a plug, I would have pulled it. There were books scattered all around me, but nothing in them I wanted to read. I scanned a dozen blogs rehashing the same political gossip, sporting news of games I'd never played and reviews of movies I'd never see. Slowly I healed and went back to work.

There were long periods when the only books I could read were things that I had already read, endlessly circling back through the same thirty or forty books that seemed to match the span of my imagination. People would tease me that the book I just recommended was the same book I had recommended a year ago, or that I could rattle off names and titles and summaries but didn't actually read anything more than reviews. Chaucer was famous for owning an extraordinary library for his time, and it only held twenty-odd books. So I thought maybe that was okay. Sometimes I couldn't read anything at all.

Just when it would start to feel like reading too was part of another life, a life I had left behind, or perhaps a life that had left me behind, I'd stumble into something that would awaken all the old feelings—immersion, alertness, awe, possibility. Zachary Mason's *The Lost Books of the Odyssey*. Frederic Prokosch's *The Asiatics*. Marguerite Yourcenar's *The Abyss*. David Markson's late novels. For the days of that discovery, I was a little bit different, as though not just flesh and bone but a little lantern as well, and sometimes one great book would make others possible and I'd submerge into a cycle of stories. But other times that door would shut again just as quickly as it opened, the book proving to be a mere spark rather than any kind of enduring flame. Then I'd rejoin the modern world in spending countless hours cruising the internet for the latest news.

It was there, online and not in one of the world's last bookstores that I first started reading about Roberto Bolaño, this mysterious figure who was virtually unknown, at least to the English world, one season and then the Next Big Thing to emerge from South America, that remote continent, dangling by a thread from the rest of the world, which has produced so much of my favorite literature. First I read his *By Night in Chile*, about a haunted Chilean priest of literary ambition, a man whose delicate sensibilities may be troubled by the violence of his times, but who becomes complicit in them, tutoring generals and sipping cognac in the homes of torturers. Then my beloved *Nazi Literature in the Americas*, where Bolaño creates an apocryphal pantheon of both comic and monstrous fascist writers, many of them frustrated poets.

Bolaño was Chilean by birth, the child of a truck driver, boxer, and schoolteacher. He was fifteen in 1968, when the whole world seemed in revolt or counter-revolt, and his family moved to Mexico City. There he quickly became active in left-wing politics and, even more hopelessly, poetry. A Trotskyist, he returned to Chile in 1973 to celebrate the presidency of Salvador Allende, but with the sudden, US-backed Pinochet coup, he was arrested and jailed. Though thousands of others who were largely indistinguishable from Bolaño were killed, and likely tens of thousands tortured, he escaped unharmed, released after just eight days by a pair of former junior high classmates who were now his prison guards—a twist so literary it's hard to entirely believe.

Back in Mexico City, Bolaño and his true friend, Mario Santiago, founded *infrarrealismo*, a poetic movement that produced very little memorable poetry but which justified shoplifting books and dealing pot and which impressed waitresses at the lowest of artist bars and, occasionally, female poets. To the extent the infrarrealists are remembered at all, it is not for their poetic works but for their provocations, which included sabotaging book readings, literary presentations, and classes to shout down or embarrass bourgeois authors. They were feared. They had a particular loathing for Octavio Paz and his followers, an animus Bolaño would later transfer to Isabel Allende. He loved picking literary fights.

In 1977, the friends traveled to Europe, where Bolaño would remain until his death in 2003. He worked odd jobs as a campground custodian, as a garbage collector, a dishwasher. He wrote poetry at night and smoked unfiltered cigarettes to the knuckle. He had lovers, fell in love, was brokenhearted and fell in love again. When his son was born, he turned to fiction, believing that he must, and that it might, provide for his family. I love that twist—who else starts writing fiction after the child is born, in order to provide for it? Only a true poet. He would submit the same story, under different titles, to multiple regional contests and collect each of their modest prizes. What had been liquor and drugs became tea. Over the last ten years of his life, starting about the same time I left for Prague but invisible to me for another decade, Bolaño churned out a handful of books that stand beside those of Borges and Marquez while dying in a quiet Costa Brava town from liver failure and inching slowly up the Everest of transplant lists.

Great work + romantic life + early death = publisher's dream. In quick succession, Bolaño's books were translated into a dozen languages and unleashed upon the world to the blaring trumpets of ecstatic reviews. When neither the thin nor fat books could sate his readers, half-finished novels and unburnt manuscripts were doctored into passible editions and heralded as essential discoveries.

Bolaño had the curious gift of being able to move effortlessly between the silly and horrific. In his 1,000-page *2666*, a black hole novel that was still sucking everything in to its unfinishable whole at his death, Bolaño begins with an absurd love quadrangle between four academics before recounting, in cataloged detail and over hundreds of pages, the brutal murders of scores of women in a thinly veiled Ciudad Juarez that are, somehow, linked to the creative emergence of the novelist Benno Von Archimboldi on the Eastern Front of World War II, whose lost nephew, it seems, may be killing some of those women himself.

Of all his books, my favorite is the most personal, *The Savage Detectives*, which describes how the grandiose delusions of youth are suffocated by middle age—which everyone knows—but also create a reserve of dignity that in our darkest moments sustains us. The first third of the book, narrated by Juan Garcia Madero, a seventeen-year-old poet, is almost too embarrassing, too ridiculous to read, and few people I've passed the book onto have managed to get past it. In heated diary prose, Garcia Madero recounts his many orgasms (today it was seven!), his entry into the Visceral Realist poetry movement facilitated by Arturo Belano and Ulises Lima, stand-ins for *infrarrealismo*, Bolaño and Santiago, the arcane late-night debates between warring poetic factions, the women he longs for and the others he beds, booze and weed.

It's fun and insufferable and trivial, and made all the more maddening by Garcia Madero's youthful capacity to take it all so seriously. But just when it seems that nothing more will happen than happens in a million adolescent fantasies every week, there's a twist of sorts, and the section ends with Garcia Madero disappearing into the Sonora desert with Belano, Lima, and Lupe, whom they are hiding from her murderous pimp, who is in hot, vengeful pursuit.

The second, much longer section is a dramatic break from the first, told as a series of forty-odd interviews conducted by an unknown character—perhaps the savage detective of the title, whatever that means—who, over twenty years, is piecing together the lives of Belano and Lima from the moment they leave Mexico City. From the Sonora Desert, they flee to Europe (for a crime only much later revealed), where their paths split with Lima adopting a life of near starvation among cruel Peruvian ex-pats in Paris, imprisonment in Israel, and among neo-Nazis in Vienna, before ultimately returning to Mexico City, while Belano settles in Spain. While that could be a story every bit as romantic as the one told by Garcia Madero, the tone is entirely different. The triumphalism is gone, and what comes across instead is how shallow our lives seem when remembered by others, mostly by people who knew us briefly, for a few days, a few months, and for whom we were more often than not minor, fleeting characters, bit players in the more essential dramas of their own narratives. What hollow ghosts we are in the realm of other peoples' memories.

The story, even as it comes to us in bits and pieces, is a hard one. The shine of youth becomes the missing teeth of middle age. There is no success, no recognition, mostly just hanging on through odd jobs and stolen books, the small, essential kindnesses of a shared meal. Even their epic friendship passes without anything so dramatic as a break, just time and distance. Lima in particular seems lost, literally disappearing into Nicaragua for two years but more essentially seeming to drift beyond any kind of intimacy with others, never finding a next self after the rebellious young poet he was, still fighting after too many years the same losing battles against Octavio Paz, which over time seem more pathetic than heroic.

But in Belano a second story starts to slowly emerge, and what could easily be read as a series of random failures and humiliations starts to assemble itself instead into a portrait of a life lived outside the norm, without reward or notice but with a rare integrity. People remember him as someone whom they could tell their secrets to. Each of the women leaves him, but often he helps them through some crisis in their lives—he is, after all, the kind of character you would only meet once your luck has run completely dry. By his mid-forties, his health was a wreck and his ambitions lost, even as he began to publish a bit. He was, increasingly, ready to die, practicing first through a ridiculous duel on a beach with a critic whom he has heard will skewer him in an upcoming review, but then, more seriously, on a journey that takes him through Angola, Rwanda, and Liberia.

This particular story is recounted by an Argentine photographer, Jacobo, who first meets Belano in Luanda, where they bond over shared affection for Cortázar and Borges. Both are on assignment for newspapers, selling Europeans stories and photos from the worst places on earth, but while Jacobo travels back and forth to Paris where he lives with his wife, Belano merely seems to shuttle between one doomed outpost and the next, descending deeper into his own death wish, a wish, Jacobo notes, that doesn't distract Belano from an obsessive regime of pharmaceuticals to ward off a host of diseases that seem perfectly capable of killing him before he'd ever do the job himself.

When their paths cross again—by utter chance and literary inevitability—they meet in a ravaged village outside of Monrovia, at the height of the Liberian Civil War, trapped between two advancing, competing rebel militias. When Jacobo arrives, Belano is already there, waiting for the worst in the company of another journalist, a Spaniard. They spend a horrible night in a shattered church, surrounded by the remaining villagers and a handful of soldiers who would never bother to protect them. Weaving in and out of delirious sleep, Jacobo listens to the Spaniard and Belano talk, and he learns the Spaniard's son has recently died, that his marriage is ruined, that he blames himself. When morning finally comes, the Spaniard decides to join a party of fleeing villagers who will all but certainly be killed on the road, a decision that clearly isn't to escape the violence but to meet it. Despite Jacobo's plea, Belano attaches himself to the Spaniard, following him out after telling Jacobo that he doesn't want to desert his friend in his hour of need.

While there are no murderous child soldiers in my jungle, every time I read that passage I feel like I'm the one walking out into the emptiness of midlife, and it frightens me—everything moving towards its end, the pleasures thinning out; the sense not that I should have done things differently but that no matter what choices I'd made, my life would have ended more or less like this. It's a hard place, but then Bolaño appears and joins me on the road. When we walk together, we talk about all sorts of things—Helena, Prague and Mexico City, about those friends who somehow had made their mark while my career plateaued, about books and the different kinds of people who write them. About the nearly unimaginable things that have been written to us on postcards. We tell each other stories—silly, tragic, sometimes redemptive—about the people we've met along the way, so many of whom we've lost. We joke about the different people we ourselves have been, but it's not a cruel laugh, something closer to wonder. How did all of that happen? We talk about our youths, so different in style but lit by similar dreams. And part of what he helps me see is my old self, my Garcia Madero, with a different kind of sympathy. Yes, I'd been ridiculous at times, and yes, I'd strayed in the mirrored temple, but I hadn't been wrong about what really matters. Then he tells me about a fantasy he has of bringing together five poets to rob a bank; they are the only companions he'd want, not safecrackers or gunmen. He's sure they'd get away with it. You wouldn't know it from looking at the two of us, he winks, but a poet's a formidable thing to have been.

TOUCHING THE VOID

"I can't believe that silly book upset you so much." The first time she said it, I assumed my mom was joking, both of us needing to trivialize the moment, but when she repeated herself just a minute or two later I started to worry that this was not just a nervous tick but perhaps the shape of her final thoughts, as though that simple gift far back in the past had formed an essential memory or held the key to some unspoken truth.

"Mom," I assured her, "that was a long time ago." But by then I'd learned all about the elasticity of time and how, especially as we age, strange, long buried moments have a way of springing into the present with alarming clarity, as if all the years in between had meant nothing at all; the past's sudden return after such a long absence made all the more unsettling by our uncertainties about yesterday or even this morning. How, as we amass time, become overwhelmed by it, the past becomes less rigid in its sequencing, forming instead some strange plastic, primordial pool through which our imaginations drift.

She was propped up against a hillside of pillows on her narrow guest bed, not wanting to die on the mattress she shared with her husband. Although it was barely wide enough for one, Helena had squeezed in beside her, wrapping Toni, who had shrunk from her already petite size into something even more fragile, in her arms. On the bedside table there was her legalistic suicide note accompanied by a stack of documents we hoped would absolve me and Helena of responsibility, a scooped-out cup of doctored pudding, an empty bottle of wine, and our glasses.

Just an hour before, the three of us had been sitting around her kitchen table, my mom and I uncoupling capsules of Seconal and tapping their deadly, sedating powder into a little dish. Like the criminal I didn't want to be, I was wearing latex gloves, which made the delicate maneuver of twirling the pill case between thumb and finger, pressing just hard enough to loosen the packed drugs without cracking the casings and sending the barbiturate everywhere, even more awkward, as did the potent combination of alcohol and adrenaline crashing through our systems. When my mom and I finally finished, I crammed the empty capsules back into the pill bottles so there would be no confusion about what had happened. My mom stirred the white powder into a store-bought container of dark chocolate pudding, mixing it thick and chalky with a spoon. By this point, I had no doubt of her resolve; the question was whether she—who squirmed at the thought of mushrooms, who gagged on the eggy scent of an omelet—could get the acidic chemical paste down and hold it there. She scooped the smallest rim, curled it under her upper lip and recoiled for a moment like a small child taking her medicine before regaining her composure. "Mmm," she smiled playfully.

A few years before, on the phone one Saturday morning, she'd told me she'd gotten some bad news. As a retiree with a capacity to imagine the worst and then fixate on it relentlessly, she'd become convinced that her memory was slipping, so she'd signed herself up for a tracking study at the University of Pennsylvania, which meant that she'd be able to establish a baseline for her brain as she drifted into her later years.

What this really meant, I immediately understood, was that she would then be able to carefully catalog each loss and tell me about it in perverse detail. From 1,000 miles away, I rolled my eyes and opened my laptop, hoping for some distraction in the nine rings of online news. If there were two things I knew about my mom, they were that she was obsessively morbid, always on the hunt for the next shard of proof that could justify her crushing anxiety, and that her memory was legendary. In time, I'd discovered these were two interlocked, mutually reinforcing traits.

She paused, suspecting my attention had wandered. "And?" I said.

And she'd gone in for her testing with a couple of friends who shared her general concerns, and while it was all very serious, it was like a game as well. They were laughing about calling their husbands by their dogs' names, about leaving the house only to pause on the doorstep, wondering where they were headed. Everyone at the testing center was elderly, everyone inching down the same fatal track. The tests themselves were administered by a small team, a nurse with a Slavic name, a couple of young assistants. That was fun too, at first, at least until the whispers and furrowed brows began to suggest there was something in her replies that troubled them. Eventually the nurse asked if my mom could stay a little longer and went to fetch the doctor, Doctor Arnold, a charming young man she thought I'd enjoy meeting at some point. Apparently she'd done well—*quite* well, she noted—on every scale but one, her short-term memory, which was not just low but belly-scraping. Rather than bringing her into the tracking study, they asked if they could do more tests, both performance based and ultimately a brain scan. She hadn't wanted to worry me with this until everything was clear, she added, but just yesterday she'd met with Doctor Arnold again and he'd delivered the diagnosis.

Ignoring my protest and questions, she added that there was something about all of this that made a kind of sense to her. Although it had begun as a game of sorts, a curiosity, she knew she'd gone in for the tests because there was something bothering her, that she had felt herself becoming a little bit less than she'd been. When the doctor said "early Alzheimer's," this strangeness inside herself suddenly had a name.

A couple weeks later we were walking, arm hooked in arm, down through the elegant, cobbled streets of old Philadelphia under a light drift of snow. We'd had a slow, sad dinner together where she reiterated her conviction, now supported by science, that her mind was tapering out, and she pushed back against any notion of experimental treatment, memory practices, or even a pragmatic assessment of slow progression and the good years she still had. She'd latched on to a dark thought from the far side; she'd found it at last. Later my aunt reminded me, "She was never going to get old."

Needing a break and feeling sentimental, we wandered to her local art cinema where we skipped the comedies and thrillers to see *Touching the Void*, a re-run documentary about a failed climb in the frozen Andes, a variation on one of her favorite themes. As is always the case, everything went wrong—a blizzard sweeps in, supplies are lost. One of the two climbers, blinded by the swirling snows, slips over an edge, hurtling down into a dark, echoing crevice. The two friends are bound by a length of rope, so the fallen man is suspended in mid-air, slowly dragging his companion, who is losing his footing on the icy rocks, down after him. That man, still on the mountain side, shouts over the edge to his friend, but between the void and the swirling winds he can't hear any reply, leaving him no way of knowing if his friend is alive or dead. Realizing he can't pull him back out and that he himself will eventually be pulled in, he makes the impossible decision to cut the rope, freeing himself but sending his friend—who was in fact alive and dangling—tumbling into the depths below, where he shatters both his legs on the rocks. From that vantage, the broken man can look up and see the sky above. He tries over and over to find a way to climb back out, but with his hands frozen and his legs useless, he accepts it is impossible. So he looks down instead, into the utter darkness at the bottom of the crevice, and decides to follow it. Down, down he goes, on broken legs, on torn hands, deeper and deeper into the darkness. Exhausted and delirious from the pain, he loses consciousness, wakes, scrambles on and on as the passage narrows, the rocks above tearing through his parka and cutting into his back, when he glimpses a little light. Finally he reaches it, a small opening way down the mountainside, and he shimmies through, back into the world. On broken legs, he somehow makes it back to their campsite, startling the friend who had left him for dead on the mountaintop.

"Listen," she said as we walked home, "I have been thinking about it a lot, you know, and I'm really quite sure the right thing for me is to end my own life once this progresses beyond a certain point.

"I know I'm muddled about some things, but I'm clear-headed on this. And strangely I don't even feel sad about it. Maybe that will come later, but I really don't feel it now. I know that I don't want to become a helpless old lady who is constantly lost, who smells bad. I hate this vision of myself with an idiotic grin on my face sitting in a pool of urine. I hate the thought of being a burden to others. Honestly, I hate the thought of whatever money I have going to pay for care I don't even want. Mostly though, I'm just okay with there being an end.

"You know, I've had 65 incredible years, an extraordinary life. I keep waiting to feel angry about something, but I just can't find any injustice to what I've been dealt. The more I think about it, I keep coming back to how outrageously fortunate I've been. At this point, all I really want is to be able to control how I die."

When I'd thought about my mom's death, which being her son I did from time to time, I'd generally imagined one of two things. If she didn't stop haranguing him, I pictured her gentle, patient husband strangling her in her sleep. More realistically, I imagined her living to be 130 years old, getting a little smaller every year but remaining relentlessly, maddeningly lucid until the end.

"Honestly," she laughed, "that's kind of how I used to picture it too. The hard part, you know, is going to be figuring out when. I can't miss that window."

I didn't try to argue her out of it. That would have been the true betrayal of the little cord that bound us, our little death seed flowering.

After a little pause she added, "I'm going to need your help."

What followed over the next few years was a strange kind of crisis: mortal but slow. Undeniable in its approach while progressing by inches. And then, every once in a while, we'd realize that something had changed, that, for example, we would come to visit and Carter was doing all of the cooking instead of my mom, the woman who'd taught so many of us what it meant to live in a kitchen. The many-layered steps of even a well-practiced recipe confused her, and that sliver of uncertainty would ruin her mood. We saw that loss of confidence in social moments that involved anyone but her closest friends. Toni, who'd always been the life of the party, suddenly hesitant to engage, uncertain of what she'd already said and resenting the thought of repeating herself. She'd excuse herself to go care for her grandkids, which had generally been the last place we'd find her. Although I continued to give her books for her birthday and Christmas, she, the consummate reader, confessed she'd all but stopped reading, discouraged by opening a book to the dog-eared page and finding herself at an utter loss for what had led her there.

When we spoke by phone or visited one another, she'd dutifully ask about the kids, of course, and add some prodding about my job, but like the true narcissist she was, she'd invariably shift the conversation to some catalog of her decline and the necessity of ending her life. In her perverse way, it made her happy to fixate on her death, to the extent she could fixate on anything. It was as though she'd finally figured out the answer to the question that had been nagging her from the start. She was always eager to talk about it. As her mind slowly crumbled around her, she could still grasp this decisive thought. We talked about when she would do it, and most elusively, how she would know the time had come.

Perhaps strangest for me was that over the course of my life I'd learned to manage my mom's anxiety—the compulsive need to not just be on time but ten minutes early, the relentless checklists of certain disasters, the presumptive despair. In fact, her obsessions had become so normalized in me that I was middle-aged before I realized I had a particular gift for befriending neurotics, for finding vitality in the wild swings of their moods and pleasure in their fixations that unnerved many others. But as the dementia took its course, she finally started to relax, as though all that anxiety depended upon a level of sustained concentration that she could rarely muster. I found her light-heartedness deeply unsettling.

She found a questionnaire that tracked the stages of Alzheimer's descent and would ask me how far I thought she had gone. "Ability to make decisions: Only some difficulty making decisions that arise in day-to-day life; Moderate difficulty, gets confused when things get complicated or plans change; Rarely makes any important decisions, gets confused easily; Not able to understand what is happening most of the time." Or, "Personal care: Takes care of self as well as they used to; Sometimes forgets to wash, shave or comb hair, or may dress in the wrong type of clothes; Requires help with dressing, washing and personal grooming; Totally depending on help for personal care." On and on, with questions that at first seemed silly but slowly felt increasingly real. She made my sister and husband answer these questionnaires as well, but she told me she didn't trust them to be honest with her; that they would underscore her losses, trying to persuade her that there was more time. She was terrified of slipping too far, of suddenly being too lost to manage the exit. She was counting on me, I was told any number of times, to tell her when her time was up.

"You don't want to have to smother me with a pillow, do you?" she'd joke when she mistakenly feared I was wavering.

A questionnaire was one thing, but even in a world of abundant, overwhelming information, clear directions on suicide are surprisingly hard to find. How was she actually going to do it? Leaping? A gun? A rope? None of that made any sense to her; it would have to be something cleaner, something medicinal. Her doctors were no help, shutting down the conversation at the first hint of its direction, and the Internet too proved unusually guarded, or she was unwilling to follow it into its darkest corners. Having quickly made peace with the abstract idea of ending her life, she was becoming increasingly desperate that she'd have no way to follow through, that there was nothing in her pill collection that would do more than make her sick. For her, the unexpected angel was a fellow traveler in her Alzheimer's group, an older psychiatrist, a widower, who was equally committed to a well-timed escape and who—no longer worried about his license, and perhaps because he had a crush on her—wrote her the deadly barbiturate prescription, which sparked days of euphoria. But when she called me next, she was in tears. "They won't fill it," she said, "they won't do it." I stepped away from the dinner table to sort out what was going on, which was fairly simple. Her pharmacist, clearly a responsible person, was refusing to fill the prescription. "Will you talk to him?" she said handing the phone over.

From a thousand miles away, I explained I was her son. Impatiently, he told me the prescription was dangerous and more likely to kill her than do any good. I paused, trying to remember what our story was. "She needs it for her back," I asserted. "Chronic pain," I mumbled. "Nothing else is helping." I could picture him looking her over.

"Do you know what you're doing?" he asked, a question for which there was no acceptable answer. When he continued to push back, I reminded him that the prescription was from her doctor and that he had a legal obligation to fill it. When he finally relented, he added, "This is going in my notes."

From *Final Exit*, we learned other details; that, for example, it's best to take a couple of antiemetics a few hours before the fatal dose itself to lessen nausea, and that it is essential to empty the drug from its capsules, as en masse they can clump together in your gut and pass before dissolving. The only part that gave her genuine pause was the insurance plan—the plastic bag over your head that, delicately propped by your thumbs, would tighten as you slipped off into sleep. While everything else seemed clean, strangely romantic, just half-real, the thought of the bag frightened her.

Only after she was gone did I realize how much my assignment allowed me to fixate on something tangible, achievable, rather than my own grief, or the anger I'd eventually feel at having been transformed into her accomplice, her sous chef, an act that would kill a bit of me as well.

* * *

She and Carter came to visit us in Minneapolis, which was always a risky affair as outside the structure of her controlled life and immersed into the chaos of a home with two working professionals and two adolescent boys anything could happen. We'd had a couple bad visits, including one where she'd gotten lost after walking a few blocks to our neighborhood store and was rescued by a kind Midwestern woman who saw another person in despair and decided to help.

Over dinner she started a story I'd never heard before, about the summer of her fifteenth birthday when her father had arranged for her stay with a Norwegian family. Together they hiked far out into the wilds, across tree-less, rocky hills, to a little cabin, which was barely visible on the horizon as it was built into a hillside and its rooftop was covered in the same sod that blanketed the terrain. She and the daughter, Anna Lise, slept on two small cots directly below the roof, and she woke in the morning to the sound of bleating and clicking bells directly above her head, with a soft dirt filtering down onto their heads.

She seemed quite alert, so I encouraged her on. She found, somewhere back in her memory, another story I'd heard long ago, but the pieces were only fragments for me and I asked her to tell it again. When my mom was ten, she was struck with such a high fever that the doctor was called to their home. After his inspection, he informed her parents that she had measles, and that she'd be sick for a few weeks. She was to be kept in her room, and her room kept dark. Her mother had to put a bright orange sign on the front door warning others that someone in the house was a danger.

She was feverish and sore, but mostly very bored. In the dark, she couldn't read, and with all the shades drawn there was nothing to see. When her father came home from work, instead of bringing books, as usual, he brought flowers, which her mother put in a vase next to the bed. Everyone, even my charmingly wicked Aunt Doug, who was only allowed to speak to her through the door, was very nice.

Her father brought her a second wind-up clock, identical to the one beside her bed, three or four screwdrivers, and a shoe box. He told Toni to have fun taking it apart, and not to worry about putting it back together again. This amused her for an afternoon, but then time started to tick on again—hour after hour in the dark. There was no telephone in the room, so she couldn't call her friends. It wasn't safe for her to go to her parents' room to watch television. Another evening her father came home with a green and brown radio, the most grown-up gift he'd ever given her. He placed it on the table next to her bed and said she was free to listen to whatever she could find. In the afternoons she followed soap operas like *Our Gal Saturday* and *As the World Turns*, and because she slept so much during the day, she was awake deep into the night. On one station she heard someone named Mario Lanza singing something that wasn't a song but instead an "aria." She couldn't understand any of the words, but was captivated by the big, rich rising and falling tones of his voice. When she told her father about it, he explained that it was "opera," a word that made her feel very grown up.

Later, when the house had been dark a long time and the radio produced mostly static, turning the dial she found—barely, faintly—a station in Wheeling, West Virginia. Its songs, sung by both men and women, were so very different from Mario Lanza's. The words were easy to understand, and full of sad stories. In the breaks between, the announcer spoke to the truckers who were driving through the night, and it gave her a different kind of grown-up pleasure to imagine herself secretly among them, a secret she kept to herself.

Though I enjoyed this track, I had work to do and as dinner wound down I suggested I lead our ritual check-in about Her Plan: did she have everything she needed, did she know what she was going to do? "Tell me," I nudged, and she did. She said she'd have a large meal, and then mix eight of her Seconal in with something to mask their flavor, applesauce or chocolate pudding. She'd take that and a big glass of wine up to her bed. With a little luck, that would do the trick.

I felt a horrible, sinking fear as she spoke—not, this time, the fear that my mom was going to die, but a very different fear that she wasn't.

"Mom," I said, "that's entirely wrong."

She looked shaken, confused. Reflexively she insisted it was me who was wrong: "I've got it written down," she asserted, but then couldn't confidently say where.

"And how many pills do you have?"

"Fifteen. I think."

"That's not going to do it. You used to have sixty. Where did they go?"

"I don't think I ever had that many."

"You did."

We were both quiet for a moment, each trying to figure out what this meant. Possibly that after all this time, all this fixation, she'd managed to lose the drugs in the back of a sock drawer or the bottom of her freezer, if not accidently thrown away. And most certainly that her ability to lay out and follow a plan, one step to the next, a simple sequence of defined actions, was passing quickly, or perhaps already gone. "Well, what am I supposed to do?"

* * *

Because she died at home, the team from the hospital where she'd agreed to donate her brain refused to take her as we'd planned and insisted that I call 911 instead. When I did, the operator urgently demanded I move her from the bed to the floor. "Why," I asked. So I could give her mouth-to-mouth. "But my mom's dead," I appealed to an unconvinced stranger.

And then the EMS crew came crashing through the house, their wide bodies up three flights of narrow stairs, only to confirm what I'd already told them. They were followed by the beat cops, who found the pill case and all her papers, who in turn were followed by the detectives, who silently, solemnly examined the evidence. "Did you know she was suicidal?" one of them asked me. "Yes," I confessed. Suddenly his posture grew erect, his attention focused, adversarial, as he sensed a crime. Why hadn't I done something about it? Why hadn't I had her hospitalized or gotten her help? Since I couldn't say, "I *was* helping," I answered, "Well, I guess because she's been suicidal for most of her life."

I was tempted to tell them about the time shortly after my parents had divorced when she'd taken herself down to the basement and somehow rigged a line to gas herself, a story that shocked me less with its intent than with the image of my mom rigging lines; she was never particularly handy. At the last moment, the will to live kicked in and she'd called friends—the Kuchars—who came to her aid and, being doctors, quickly focused on any meds she'd been taking. It didn't take long to realize she'd just started a different anti-depressant that week, a change of chemicals that had destabilized her highly reactive mind.

As I spoke with the detective, I was looking across the room at a photo I'd given her from a dog-sledding trip we'd taken one winter in far northern Minnesota. She's at the back of the sled, ready to launch Into the Wild, with a serious, commanding look on her face, completely able, four half-rabid dogs already lunging against her grip on the reins. Fear and adventure, despair and command—all that in one little body.

The detectives were followed in turn by the Crime Scene Investigators, who I thought only existed on TV. They had more questions about what we knew and when, where we had been. We descended into an odd kind of dance, a charade, where everyone must have known what had happened—that the family of an elderly, demented woman had at a minimum allowed her to kill herself or possibly helped. None of the inspectors seemed eager to pass judgment on that, as that would require them to act; no one wanted to dig too deep, but they also needed me to lie and confess my utter surprise so that they could wrap up their paperwork and leave. Until then, there remained a vague possibility that Helena and I would end up in cuffs. Everything that should have been grief was smothered by fear. At one point when I, tired and upset, started to stray from the script, one of them, the most senior among them, the kind one, took me out of the room and said, "Please don't say any more."

The day of her death itself had been so different. We'd been nervous then too, of course, but it was a private fear rather than one shared with uniformed strangers. We had wanted the day to last forever until we got a taste of what that really meant—each minute dragging on and on, little tortured eternities. We walked to the river and sat in the sun. We drank coffees and tea. We wandered through her house. We made an early lunch no one wanted to eat. She tried to make small talk. We drank a bit, read every article in the *Times*. We tried to talk seriously, but what more was there to say? We flipped through magazines and art books. I tried to fill my mind with memories but found very little I could hold. We went for another walk. I took a long bath, just to be alone, shivering with nerves. She and Carter spoke.

It was a strange, guilty relief when the time finally came. And for a moment, for a little last window, she was her old, best self again, leading the way, even slightly giddy as if setting off on a grand adventure, the way a certain blend of fear and adrenaline can make you laugh a bit too easily.

Trapped somewhere between a fear of her death and a fear of the law, my sister and step-father said their impossible good-byes and left. After the mixing was done, Helena and I took Toni up to her bed and settled her in. Helena, always a bit more human than I, curled in beside her. She spooned down the pudding, wincing a bit but never wavering, then washed her mouth with red wine to cleanse the chemical sting. The drugs were moving fast. When she looked up and saw me, she shook her head just a little and asked again, "You know I never thought of you as cowardly?"

"I know, mom, but let's talk about something else."

I tried to think of something.

"Do you remember once telling me that in midlife you had four ambitions: to lead a dog-sled, to cross the Sinai on camel, to speak another language fluently, and to learn to tango."

She smiled at that. "Not really, but it sounds like me."

After a long pause that made me wonder what she was tracking, she added, "I didn't quite get there but I guess I did all right."

"Can you picture Ossabaw?" I asked.

She could. She remembered the large colonies of mussels clinging to the dock when the little boat arrived from the mainland, the smell of salt water. In that same bay, when the moon had pulled the tide to its limits, the artists would wade into the shallows, digging with their feet until they felt the smooth firmness of clamshells. After toeing them out, they'd hold the clams aloft in the moonlight then drop them back into the wet sand bed. She closed her eyes but continued, a little slower, a little less clearly than before. One night, maybe it was her last one there, she heard a rhythmic sighing sound out beyond the marsh, and she could just make out a pod of dolphins moving up the coast. She stayed there in the shallows watching as they passed out of sight.

ELSEWHERES

I assembled a few objects scavenged from her home around my desk—a boar's skull and turtle bone; a long, bent Roman nail; a silver bracelet from Mali; a cast bronze cage built around a little figure on a swing; her father's sterling silver champagne debubbler. On the wall, I hung a picture of her Ossabaw tree house and another of her astride a bicycle in the Valley of the Kings. Her ashes sat, in an unexpectedly large plastic bag, on the top shelf of my closet.

Back at work it was my colleague Astrid, an extraordinarily pale woman from finance with lightly curled hair and wind-chapped cheeks, a woman with whom I'd barely ever exchanged more than a nod or passing hello, who surprised me by being the most able to sit beside me and not just offer condolences but to ask about Toni's life, what she'd done, how she'd chosen to die, what my kids did and didn't understand about her choice. Others I knew much better circled around me uncertainly, as though fearing contagion.

Like my boss, a close friend with whom I'd drunk late into the night and in half a dozen cities from coast to coast, someone with whom I'd provoked and narrowly avoided a string of edifying disasters, who couldn't come anywhere near me. My first day back, I startled him like a ghost. He quickly shook my hand, fumbled a few words of official sympathy while looking over my shoulder and made an excuse to cut away. The next day I found a note he left on my desk expressing his "sadness at the passing of Mrs. Hamilton." I started to loathe him, and then work, which had been a refuge, a pleasure and a purpose for many years, became something bitter. Or maybe I did.

There is a William Stafford poem about keeping a journal that I've read jealously many times over the years. He describes the intimate act of organizing his thoughts in those pages, evening after evening, one beside the other, and how there "everything / recognized itself and passed into meaning." From a dark recess of my basement, I retrieved a plastic container box holding twenty-five volumes of my diaries, ranging from the simplest schoolboy notebooks to elegant, fine press treasures that always seemed too exquisite for my thoughts, some filled to the final margin while others trail off mid-point. The most recent were more than ten years old. I re-read them all that winter, hoping that I'd be transported back into the past and rediscover some secret knowledge that had since been lost, but mostly I found myself skimming along. A great deal was recorded but not much passed into meaning. A record of days and places, names, small events, small emotions, petty wounds, misspelled words. So often the most interesting stories, the true stories, belonged to someone else.

Without ever having given it much thought, I had apparently internalized the expectation that I'd live deep into my 90s, a proxy for a very long time from now. But my mom had died young, or at least at an age that now seemed young to me, and Alzheimer's had been eating away at her mind for some years prior to that. If that were the case for me, perhaps I only had another fifteen good ones left. A blink. Then I'd do the same. Final exit.

Maybe, I thought, as I'm sure my dad had once thought too, maybe my boys will put it all together and punch a hole in the sky.

When the ground softened in the spring, Helena and I planted a pear tree above her ashes.

If I read anything at all during that time, it had to be short and dark, espresso-like, like Javier Sandoval's novella *Ithaca*, about a Caribbean islander in the early days of the New World apocalypse. The story takes place years after the Spaniards first lured him from his fishing canoe aboard their ship, tricked him into cuffs and brought him to Castile. So many, in fact, that when he finally does return (alone—the others have all died) his

fellow islanders assume, no matter what he says, that he must be a ghost
sent to haunt them. By then, his wife has become his brother's wife and
his kids his brother's kids. As disturbing as his presence is, they can't bring
themselves to chase him away because he is, after all, *their* ghost. So they
allow him to linger in the woods around their village and on the rocks
of their bay, surviving on the little offerings of fish or smoked snake the
children bring him.

Mostly the children scurry away as fast as they can when he appears,
laughing and playfully frightened by his unnatural presence, but some
nights he is able to lure one of his sons, the eldest, into staying with him
around the dying fire by promising to tell him stories of the other world,
which he calls Spain but the boy knows must be Death. The boy likes to
hear about the great battles, the great warriors, the grand queen and her
court, of the gods and their childish whims. The father, however, prefers
a tale he heard on one of his many ships of a clever sailor who, after a long
war between the Spanish and their Trojan foes, begins a ten-year voyage
home full of misadventure, battles of wit and betrayal, monsters and lost
companions. In the end, he assures his son and digging a stick into their
fire, everything is set right.

It was a little book, published by a little press, by a lovely writer whom
almost no one knew, and I suppose I considered it my own in some way.
If I wasn't going to write something like that myself, I could at least be
a collector of sorts, a reader of uncommon taste. So I was doubly taken
aback or perhaps just disappointed the next winter when drifting through
The Los Angeles Review of Books I came upon an interview with my old
antagonist Geoffrey Bannon, in which he heralded *Ithaca* as among his
favorite discoveries.

I had followed his career of course but had thought it best not to read
him. His first book, *his* Prague story, had made him a minor star while
still in his mid-twenties, which at one point filled me with jealousy but
which I also came to recognize as a difficult gift. In its reviews, he claimed
to have written it in a twelve-week fever in a cabin in Maine, "after fleeing
the continent," on a diet of oysters, whiskey, and cigarettes, despite his

sparkling white teeth. People loved that ridiculous claim, of course, at least for a moment, but almost as soon as he'd seized the Zeitgeist, it slipped out of his spidery hands. The young ones just after him thought Prague passé and headed instead for Moscow, Beijing, or Dubai. The stories they told glittered with devices and artificial intelligences.

He could easily have been a one-trick thirty-year-old. No one much cared for his rehashed second novel, but after a silence, I don't really know how long it was, he started to publish again, a couple of novels—a crime story in which the damsel, despite evidence to the contrary, insists she's dead; something about islands—that were rarely reviewed, and modestly then, almost always with some reference back to his early promise. Sometimes one would appear on the long list for some second-tier award or another.

Every few years, just when he'd begin to be forgotten, replaced, some new title would appear, often with a different publisher. His most recent was a thicker novel called *Elsewheres*. I'd heard it was a story about lost cities, fake books, and swapped identities—three of the things that had always interested me the most. It had always felt like a betrayal of something, my own possibilities I suppose, to read him, but whatever I'd once felt had become watery and thin a long time ago. At the college bookstore near my house, I bought a copy, which then sat beside my bed for several weeks or maybe a month before I finally relented.

In a brief, pseudo-academic prologue, he sets our story up: having crossed the Pacific, tracked the Nile to its source, opened the Northwest Passage, and cracked China, the European expansion is turning its attention to the next great void of its map—the Sahara. Educated gentlemen in the geological societies of London and Paris come to blows speculating on its oases and wonders. When a fresh letter from this Edge of the World arrives, it is cause for headlines and café chatter. Some Frenchmen have begun to plot a great trans-Saharan train line that will connect their fledgling colony in Algeria to the gold, salt, and ivory markets of remote Timbuktu, if only they can figure out just where it is. That's the question. The prize.

At the northern rim of the desert, there exists in a world of European agents, soldiers, and merchants, men slowly adding a village *here*, a well *there*, a mountain pass *there* to Europe's maps. Over the last several decades, the French have brought Algeria under their nominal thumb, but beyond Algiers itself and a few fortified camps, different laws still reign. Not many have ventured farther than the desert's lip before they were chased out by thirst or natives—the Tuareg, those fierce, blue-skinned raiders with a penchant for murdering anyone who trespassed on their unfathomable wasteland.

One place these men sometimes meet at is a trading post in Brezina, across the coastal plains and down the Atlas Mountains from Algiers, supplying Arab farmers and Berber nomads. To the east and west, small farms profitably grow wheat, cotton, and tobacco. To the south, the desert and whatever treasure it holds. The trading post is home to a shopkeeper and his son.

Nothing at all has happened for weeks or months on end, but one evening the son hears a heavy thump outside their door, and when he steps outside he sees a Berber cameling away. There is, however, a man crumpled at the boy's feet. Though the stranger looks dead, the boy knows no one would bother to deliver him here if he were. When father and son lift him by feet and arms, they are shocked by how light he is, just skin and bones under his canvas shirt and pants. As they knock him through the uneven doorway, a leather notebook falls from the folds of his robe.

While the boy cares for their guest, the father pours himself a drink and settles down by lamplight with the stranger's journal. Flipping through the early pages, he learns the man's name, that he is a native of Nice, and how he'd set off for his grand adventure of Africa. "Why are we not just bored but outraged when others veer into cliché," Geoffrey asks, "as though they are attempting to steal something for themselves that belongs to us all?" What the journal reveals is a universal plot, the variable stuff of young lives: the tearless goodbye to the hardscrabble family, the older brother only too relieved to see him go. Rough seas. Overwhelmed on the docks by the foreign voices, the clawed hands. The thrill of escape into this vast, uncharted world, its endless, unattainable possibilities. The woman who looks you in the eye, lingers there. Doubts, followed by exaggerated claims, by doubts.

As the father reads through this over-told story, he knows he could have written the same naive words himself almost twenty years earlier. When he arrived in a fierce land across a sea, he faced all those hardships too, but he did it with a wife and their first child in tow. A comfort at times perhaps, but as often a burden while he tried to negotiate these strange markets, to establish some foothold. He had something more than his own life to lose. He's often wondered where he could have gone without them. Perhaps rather than settling for the life of a shopkeeper, he'd have set out himself—into the desert, onto history's page. But that's not the way it happened. They were a family. He opened a shop. They scratched by. He lived, as did his second son. Years passed.

The father turns the pages roughly, as though he might shake the idiocy of youth from the stranger. But the father reads on, trusting that events themselves will humble him, and in some modest ways they do. Learning Arabic is more of a struggle than the stranger had imagined. In the bazaar, he's swindled by a pair of merchants. One night he gets lucky at cards, only to be roughed up by the soldiers whose pay he'd won. He knows Algiers is eating him up, but rather than turn back, he decides to go farther.

The stranger joins a caravan headed south, everything is south, but somewhere between El Bayadh and Ghardaia the nomads he is traveling with rob and beat him. Left for dead, he lives. With no hope of going back, he tracks the bandits, but loses their trail in the dunes. Hot hours, silvery days pass. When he first sees the Tuareg, he's not sure if they are real or mirages—quivering on the horizon, disappearing, emerging on the next ridge. Eventually he collapses and awakes, hands bound, slung across a camel's back.

As the stranger's mind slowly returns, he wonders why they don't kill him. Because a single man, just barely a man, is hardly a threat? Because they intend to sell him as a slave? Because they enjoy watching him suffer and have barely begun? Because some guardian, this warrior or that girl, has taken pity on him? Two days later, they untie his wrists. There is no need for chains: the desert is a limitless cell.

They travel mostly at night, guided by stars. They cross mountain ranges, empty riverbeds, vast plateaus of shattered black rock. Enormous fossilized bones (of what impossible beast?) jut up out of the earth, white in the scorching sun. On some stretches, stiff, grey-green grasses break through the sand, like a thousand little spears. From the Tuareg, he learns the Sahara is not a single desert but many, each with its own secret borders and distinctions.

Beyond Ouargla they raid an Arab camp, stealing a sack of dates, a necklace with a solid silver pendant, a musket, and three goats. They may have killed a man. In Illizi, they trade the dates for a dried cattle skin. Some days later, a sand storm sweeps across the plains. They barely escape after roping everyone and their beasts together. He writes that he'll never forget the sound of a camel screaming through the wind, though he never mentions it again.

In time, he writes, he learns the rudiments of the nomad tongue, but he's careful not to ask too much about their route, knowing they'd slit a spy's throat. He records the names of its signposts—this ridge, that rock formation—and notes the directions and distances between them in the sweeping generalizations of "three nights by camel."

Near Tamanrasset they join two other clans, relatives perhaps, though the connections are hard to unwind, for a fortnight of camel races, roast goat and courtship. The women go unveiled, while the men wrap their heads in indigo cloth. Another theory emerges on why he is still alive: they like exotic pets. Under the stars, an old man plucks a one-stringed violin and sings the history of the Tuareg people.

Around a dung fire he tries, using his handful of words, a few props, a stick in the sand, to describe the world he increasingly suspects he'll never see again: glass, snow, cathedrals, fish. He fantasizes how one of these fantastic, alien objects may take root in Tuareg mythology and emerge, even generations later, in some new form. I wasn't the only one, apparently, who'd read too much Calvino.

After many weeks, a child's death, a plague of flies, the desert ends, or gives way to something else. Rough, then gentler grasslands spread, supporting cattle and larger villages, although the Tuareg mostly avoid them. It may be February when he first sees Timbuktu. His companions, they've become that now, warn him that as a Christian he'll be killed if he enters this holy city, but they also take some evident pleasure in draping him in Tuareg cloth and critiquing his imitation of their camel-inflicted walk.

He can hardly believe the noises and scents of Timbuktu. Everything seems to run over, spill out of itself. You bump shoulders with a stranger in a crowded market and walk away with his smell in your nose, his words in your head. Three great mosques made of packed mud and wooden beams tower upwards, dominating the city. Everything else is flat. Ivory tusks, ostrich eggs. In the slave market, he sees black Africans chained for the coast. There are no Portuguese, but their goods—beads, axes, iron belt buckles—are scattered throughout the bazaar. Manuscripts too. He's told it is a city with one hundred libraries, collecting the countless Islamic books on astronomy, botany, music, law, and history. "Salt comes from the earth," someone tells him. "Gold from the south, but the word of God and treasures of wisdom come from Timbuktu."

This is not, to say the least, what the father was expecting to read—that this foolish stranger would be the one who finally did it, who discovered the hidden city, and even lived. It occurs to him that in his entire life he's probably never held anything as valuable as these dry pages, brittle pages worth more than gold. Buried beneath the stranger's xenomania and self-dramatization are the simple yeses and nos, the days, directions, and names, that people—very important people—are waiting to hear. The book itself is a road from Algiers to Timbuktu, a key to the treasure trove.

For the first time in many years, the father is conscious of wanting something. He wants the money, for sure. He's owed it—for two dead kids, a buried wife, a collapsing lung, his last boy stranded here on the rim of nowhere. But he wants more than the money. He wants for all of this to have been worth something, for there have been some purpose to all the loss. He wants the book to be his, to be the story of *his life*, as though he could just slip into its covers like another skin.

The father knows he's not crossing any deserts at this point, but what if this stranger died? He very well might. And what if the father took the book and disappeared for a while, a season or so? It would be easy to do. His son could manage the shop while he re-wrote the book, in his own hand and voice (although borrowing some of its better phrases), bringing maturity and perspective to it, some calm, while retaining all that the stranger had learned. And then, when enough time had passed, he'd emerge—not deliriously dumped on a doorstep, but looking every bit as worn—and take what's his.

Which begged the next question: why leave it to chance? Why let some fever decide whether or not he has a future? He could do it that night, after his son went to bed. It might even be kind. He'd seen cases like this before, where someone survives meningitis, but their brain's been stripped to its core. He tightens his fist, imagining the stranger's frail throat. He squeezes until the joints of his fingers throb, but no matter how ruthless he dreams he's become, he knows he won't take this next step. More tired than brutal, unable to sustain even the fantasy of wealth and fame, unable to convince himself it could be any more than a fantasy. It is another journey he might have made ten, fifteen years ago, but not now. One look at him and they—the journalists, the mapmakers, the capitalists, the women— would know he never could have made it to Timbuktu and back, that that kind of journey just wasn't in him.

The novel's second section shifts its focus from the father to the stranger, whose feverish body has been little more than a prop so far. At last, he wakes. Of course, he has no idea where he is, how he got there, only a vague idea of who he is. A boy explains how they found him, how they have watched over him these days, dripping well water down his throat. It doesn't make any sense. The stranger remembers: a blue moonlit night when he could see for miles through the darkness, goat grease on his hands, the sickening rock of a camel's gait. And then he falls back into his darkness.

When he wakes the second time, he thinks he's slept twenty years— the boy is now a man, worn and tough. Then he realizes his mistake. "Remember this?" the father asks, dropping a notebook on his lap. The man seems to hate him already, which doesn't particularly surprise the stranger. People do. When he takes the book in his hands, it's like touching one end of a long golden thread that might, just possibly, lead him back through the labyrinth.

Rather than comforting him, however, the book only deepens his disorientation. While the first pages take him back to his arrival in Algiers, it's not long before he starts to sense a divergence between the stories this book tells and what he actually remembers. In his journal, a woman returns his slow gaze and he rhapsodizes about what might have been. But what he remembers is following her back to her room. When she demanded to be paid, he slapped her and she screamed, perhaps in pain or shock but more likely to summon her pimp. In a panic, he raced back to the cover of the streets, triumphant and scared. In his journal, a string of luck allows him to take a week's pay from four soldiers at cards. He bought round after round of drinks. When he stumbled home, the four men jumped him on the street. But what he remembers is the moment when they caught him nicking the deck, how they extracted their slow revenge.

Now it comes back to him. It was no better in the caravan he joined, which he did less to go further than to escape the place he was in. As soon as the last town faded from sight, he was shaking with dread, with the knowledge that sooner or later his companions would turn on him, eat him alive or leave him for dead. For some reason he couldn't understand—his mastery of the language was poor, worse than he'd imagined setting out—they betrayed one of their own instead, a frail Arab who, even to this stranger, was clearly a thief, though to be honest he couldn't tell if it was justice or entertainment that began with taunts and ended with camel whips and knives. The others divvied up his goods. He thought about making a run for it—but to where? There was only one unmarked way, and they were on it together. He tried to befriend other traders, to build some shaky alliances, but they kept their distance, as though they didn't want to be tangled up in his unlucky fate.

Eventually he remembers the truth, or as close as he can get to it: that what began as a journal, as some half-honest reckoning of his days, quickly became something else—a place where he could play out the elaborate fantasy that increasingly diverged from his actual path. In Geoffrey's words,

"His pen scratched a narrow opening on the page, a crevice of ink. He stepped through it and went on." His first entries were sprawling as he pushed out the boundaries of this new territory, filled with strange foods and unlikely objects, secret passes, flowering oases, beautiful Tuareg girls and their dignified, dangerous fathers.

When, at the end of a ride, the men gathered in their tents and swapped their tales, he'd sit quietly behind them, hoping to pick up some thread—a curious tale that would begin another story, the first line of a new chapter. But most of what they had to say was the simple, eternal exchange of merchant news: in Sidi Bel Abbes, there was a shortage of salt; in Medea, the apricot crop had failed.

The fever must also have been lingering at the back of one of their tents, or perhaps in the cool shadow of a desert well. Like a hunter, it went for the weakest of the pack. The reader is left to assume that it was some member of the caravan who left the fever-wrecked stranger on the shop's doorstep.

The third and final section of *Elsewheres* is the briefest. Having given the father and stranger their due, Geoffrey shifts his narrative to the son, who opened the door at the novel's start but then stepped aside, allowing the two older men to lead. I kept wondering which of the three Geoffrey most identified with, but of course that was the wrong question. What he'd created were all just shifting versions of the same person, or empty vessels to be filled with plot as their stories were traded back and forth.

Given how reticent he'd been, it is something of a surprise to find the son has a voice, and that—within his head at least—it is neither meek nor tame. He has read the journal too, mostly while the stranger slept. For his entire life the desert, which begins just south of their homestead, has been the horizon, and he's carried with him a sense of shame that although no barrier or gate had blocked his way, he'd allowed himself to be barred from it. He doesn't hate his father, but sees him for what he is—broken, heavy, finished. Though the father believes he is providing for his son, the boy knows he is the one who holds them together. It is a life where nothing ever happens. And then something did.

With the certainty only an adolescent can sustain, the son knows that although the stranger would swear he wrote the book for the great merchants of Paris, he would be wrong. The stranger wrote it for him. And destiny, or The Desert if you'd rather call it that, coughed the stranger up on this door so that this boy could take the book and follow it. While this might be the end of the older men's adventures, it is only the beginning of his. In the middle of the night, he wakes silently and steals from the house, taking the notebook and his father's nag. He's already plotted his course to Timbuktu, back through the stranger's wandering. He knows the signposts, the oases, even the names of the traders he'll trust or avoid. The book is his map, and if he follows it closely enough, somehow its story will become his own, "its roads indistinguishable from his veins."

The end, those last ecstatic pages as the son saddles up and rides through the dark hours before dawn, is perfectly ambiguous, which I assume is what Geoffrey wanted. The contrast between what the son believes, that fortune awaits him, and what the reader knows, that he's setting off into a devouring desert guided by a map that is nothing more than seductive fiction, is the stuff of tragedy, but as the morning rises it is a glorious day and the next chapter is unwritten.

Acknowledgements

The Thirteenth Month draws heavily on various other books I would like to acknowledge, including Bruno Schulz's *The Cinnamon Shops* (Celina Wieniewska, translator), Lawrence Durrell's *The Alexandria Quartet*, Roberto Bolaño's *The Savage Detectives* (Natasha Wimmer, translator), C.P. Cavafy's *Collected Poems* (Rae Dalvin, translator), Italo Calvino's *Invisible Cities* (William Weaver, translator), Fernando Pessoa's *The Book of Disquiet* (Margaret Jull Costa, translator), Jack Gilbert's *Monolithos* and *The Great Fires*, Rainer Maria Rilke's *The Selected Poetry of Rainer Maria Rilke* (Stephen Mitchell, translator), Mark Strand's *Reasons for Moving*, and Jorge Luis Borges' stories and essays (Andrew Hurley, Eliot Weinberger, Esther Allen, Suzanne Jill Levine, Anthony Kerrigan, and others, translators).

The majority of the first chapter, "Call It Courage," first appeared in *The Rumpus*. The majority of the final chapter, "Elsewheres," first appeared in *The Chicago Quarterly Review*.

Permissions

Colin Hamilton has helped create libraries, artist housing projects and a center for dance. He now works in public media. *The Thirteenth Month* is his first novel and follows a poetry chapbook. He lives in St. Paul.